"TOUCH THAT GUN AND I'll KILL YOU!"

Silence followed Reno's warning. Then the men slowly lifted their arms away from their guns. Rand, the saloon owner, swiveled his chair around to face Reno.

"What the hell do you want?" he demanded.

"If you ever try shanghaiing another girl for your bawdy house upstairs, or I hear of you rolling a drunk, or one of these hired guns tricks a man into a shootout, I'll burn this damn place to the ground." And, when Rand's expression didn't change, Reno added, "And I want these two-bit gunhawks gone by morning."

"You're overstepping yourself," Rand protested. "I don't have to—"

Reno let his hand hang suggestively by his holster. "You have to," he said, "unless you'd rather bury them . . ."

 Signet Brand Western

BR

SIGNET Westerns by Ray Hogan

(0451)

- ☐ **THE LAW AND LYNCHBURG** (121457—$2.25)*
- ☐ **THE RENEGADES** (119282—$2.25)*
- ☐ **DECISION AT DOUBTFUL CANYON** (111192—$1.95)*
- ☐ **THE DOOMSDAY BULLET** (116305—$1.95)*
- ☐ **THE DOOMSDAY TRAIL** (093542—$1.75)
- ☐ **THE HELL RAISER** (094891—$1.75)*
- ☐ **LAWMAN'S CHOICE** (112164—$1.95)*
- ☐ **OUTLAW'S PLEDGE** (097785—$1.95)*
- ☐ **PILGRIM** (095766—$1.75)*
- ☐ **RAGAN'S LAW** (110307—$1.95)*
- ☐ **THE RAPTORS** (091248—$1.75)
- ☐ **SIGNET DOUBLE WESTERN: OUTLAW MARSHAL and WOLF LAWMAN** (117441—$2.50)*
- ☐ **SIGNET DOUBLE WESTERN: MAN WITHOUT A GUN and CONGER'S WOMAN** (120205—$2.95)*
- ☐ **SIGNET DOUBLE WESTERN: BRANDON'S POSSE and THE HELL MERCHANT** (115910—$2.50)
- ☐ **SIGNET DOUBLE WESTERN: THE DEVIL'S GUNHAND and THE GUNS OF STRINGAREE** (093550—$1.95)
- ☐ **SIGNET DOUBLE WESTERN: LAWMAN FOR SLAUGHTER VALLEY and PASSAGE TO DODGE CITY** (091736—$1.95)*
- ☐ **SIGNET DOUBLE WESTERN: THREE CROSS and DEPUTY OF VIOLENCE** (116046—$2.50)
- ☐ **SIGNET DOUBLE WESTERN: DAY OF RECKONING and DEAD MAN ON A BLACK HORSE** (115236—$2.50)*

*Prices slightly higher in Canada

THE LAW
AND
LYNCHBURG

by
Ray Hogan

Ⓢ
A SIGNET BOOK
NEW AMERICAN LIBRARY
TIMES MIRROR

PUBLISHER'S NOTE

This novel is a work of fiction. Names, characters, places, and incidents are either the product of the author's imagination or are used fictitiously, and any resemblance to actual persons, living or dead, events, or locales is entirely coincidental.

NAL BOOKS ARE AVAILABLE AT QUANTITY DISCOUNTS WHEN USED TO PROMOTE PRODUCTS OR SERVICES. FOR INFORMATION PLEASE WRITE TO PREMIUM MARKETING DIVISION, THE NEW AMERICAN LIBRARY, INC., 1633 BROADWAY, NEW YORK, NEW YORK 10019.

 SIGNET TRADEMARK REG. U.S. PAT. OFF. AND FOREIGN COUNTRIES
REGISTERED TRADEMARK—MARCA REGISTRADA
HECHO EN CHICAGO, U.S.A.

SIGNET, SIGNET CLASSICS, MENTOR, PLUME, MERIDIAN AND NAL BOOKS are published by The New American Library, Inc., 1633 Broadway, New York, New York 10019

First Printing, March, 1983

1 2 3 4 5 6 7 8 9

PRINTED IN THE UNITED STATES OF AMERICA

☆ **1** ☆

Magatagan came through the swinging doors of the Yellow Jacket Saloon, shoulders rigid, hatred glowing in his dark eyes. There was an icy single-mindedness to him, and men standing nearby, whether or not in his direct path, stepped aside, giving him wide passage.

Reaching the center of the street, he started for its lower end in a hurried, purposeful stride, looking neither right nor left. A fairly tall, muscular man, he moved with an easy grace that reflected the perfect coordination of his lank body.

"Who's that?" one of several men standing in front of the close-by Las Vegas Bank wondered in a cautious sort of way.

"Name's Magatagan—Reno Magatagan," the man next to him replied in an equally careful tone. "Seen him up in Wichita a time ago. He's a real bad one."

"Can tell that just from looking at him. What do you reckon he wants here?"

"Don't know, but he was talking to old Jake, who used to drive a stagecoach for the Overland outfit before he got all busted up in a wreck, in the saloon earlier this morning. Seemed to be asking him questions about something—or maybe somebody."

"Somebody he's out to kill—"

1

"Ain't no doubt about that. I'm wondering who."

Magatagan heard only the sound of the words being spoken as he passed by, caught none of their meaning. His attention was riveted to a building on his left and a hundred feet or so on ahead. LOCKLEAR'S GENERAL STORE the sign on the false front of the flat-roofed structure read. Magatagan's jaw tightened even more, and the corners showed white beneath the deep brown of his skin. It had taken a long time—a good ten years, in fact—to track down Henry Bigbee, mostly because the man, he'd just learned, had changed his name. But the search was now over, was ending here in this high-meadow town of New Mexico Territory.

Talk along the street died completely as more persons along its dusty way caught sight of Magatagan's taut figure. A dog wandered out from the passageway lying between the Chinese Laundry and Beacon's Saddle Shop, and halted when he saw the approaching gunman. Caught up also by the sudden tension, the mongrel began to back away, barking furiously, the hair on its neck lifting.

Magatagan, paying no heed, pressed relentlessly on, his narrowed eyes fixed on the doorway of Locklear's, now only a short distance away. At that moment a woman in front of Swartz's Meat Market, adjacent to the general store, paused, then, taking a tighter grip on the hand of the child with her, hurried off.

"It's Locklear's he's headed for," a voice ventured quietly from the men gathered in front of the bank. "You reckon it's Nat he's after?"

"Who else?" someone countered. "Nat ain't got nobody working in there but him."

Magatagan's steps slowed. His right hand dropped

to the pistol hanging on his hip, came to rest lightly on the weapon's worn butt. At the same time his left hand raised, brushed back the battered hat he was wearing as if to remove any possible impediment to his view.

Near the front of the building he veered from a straight course and slanted toward the three steps leading up to the store's landing, cluttered with stacks and piles of water buckets, washtubs, horse collars, harnesses, and various other articles currently in demand. Coming to the steps, Magatagan mounted them slowly, glance now whipping back and forth across the front windows and the entrance to the building as if to make certain he was not facing an ambush. Halting at the screened door, he pulled it open and hastily stepped inside to prevent any silhouetting.

"Bigbee! Henry Bigbee!" The gunman's voice could be heard the length of the hushed street. "I'm Dave Magatagan's son. Been hunting you ever since Willow Creek. I've come to settle up for what you done to my pa. You hear me, Bigbee?"

There was a long silence, and then from somewhere in the shadowy depths of the building the storekeeper replied.

"My name ain't Bigbee!"

"Too late for lying. I talked to a man who remembered seeing your name on some papers he brought you. You've come to the end of your rope. Time to settle up."

There was no response to that. Magatagan repeated his words in part, and gun out and ready, he walked deeper into the store. He halted abruptly when the sound of the rear door closing softly reached him. Bigbee had slipped out the back. Pivoting swiftly, Magatagan returned to the landing, deeming it not only unwise but foolish to follow the merchant and thereby expose himself.

Again outside the building, Magatagan dropped from the landing and took up a stand off to one side, where he was afforded a good view of the store. Unless he was mistaken, Bigbee would circle the structure, hoping to take him from behind.

Motionless in the driving sunlight, Magatagan waited. A dark, unsmiling man, he was wearing a faded red shirt, a leather vest that once was black but now weathered to gray, colorless cord pants, scarred stovepipe boots, and a yellow neckerchief that had belonged to a member of the United States cavalry stationed at Colorado's Fort Collins. He preferred his mustache full and usually went without a beard unless it was inconvenient to shave. He was a Kentuckian by birth, but his family had moved to Kansas while he was small. There he grew up, served his stint in the war when it broke out, returning after Appomattox, and a time later setting out to track down Henry Bigbee.

"Ain't somebody going to get the marshal?" a voice coming from somewhere nearby wondered. "We ought to stop this here killing."

Magatagan, hand again resting on the butt of his .44, turned toward the source of the words—a group of a half-dozen bystanders gathered beneath a cottonwood that was spreading its shade over the street.

"Forget it," he said in a flat, cold way. "You'll only get him killed, too. My quarrel's only with Bigbee."

"Why? What'd he do to you?"

"Can't see as it's any put-in of yours, but he let my pa die—double-crossed him—let him rot in the stinking pen so's he could go scot-free—"

Magatagan's words broke off abruptly. Motion near a shed behind the store building had caught the corner of an eye. His hand came up swiftly, little more than a blur. The weapon he held sent its echoing blast along the rows of structures facing one another across the street, setting the dogs to barking and startling a dozen or so pigeons roosting on the roof of the Elms Hotel into noisy flight.

Magatagan, slumped forward, smoke curling lazily about his taut shape, continued to watch the wavering figure near the shed. A thickset, round-faced man in dusty serge pants and linsey-woolsey shirt and wearing a denim bib apron, he staggered forward, one hand clutching the rifle he had raised to fire, the other now braced against the side of the small shed as he sought to support himself. He managed two uncertain steps, and then releasing his grip on the rifle, fell facedown on the warm, loose soil.

Magatagan, reloading, moved slowly to where he was beside the prostrate figure. Then, using his booted foot, he rolled the man over onto his back. Several of the bystanders eased up for a closer look. Magatagan turned to the one on his right.

"He the one you call Locklear?"

The man nodded. "Yessir, Nat Locklear. Is—was the owner of—"

He fell silent. Magatagan had wheeled, was striding back down the street toward his horse, which was waiting at the rack in front of the Yellow Jacket Saloon.

... ...

☆ **2** ☆

Midway along the street Reno Magatagan slowed
his steps. A hard grin pulled at his mouth. Directly
ahead and hurrying toward him was a man wearing a
star. The town marshal.

"Hold up there, Magatagan," the lawman shouted, raising a hand, palm forward.

The gunman's lips tightened. The marshal knew
who he was. That wouldn't help matters any.

"What was that shooting about? You mixed up in
it?"

The lawman, a tall, lean man with smooth, youthful features, came to a stop. He was lucky, Reno
thought, to be up against a town marshal rather than
a sheriff. The latter, because of their greater authority, were always much harder to handle.

"Could be," Magatagan replied.

"He killed Nat Locklear," a man in the crowd
trailing the gunman volunteered. "Shot him down—"

"Was a fair fight, Tom. Nat had a rifle," someone
else added.

The marshal hawked, spat into the dust. "It ain't
ever no different where Magatagan's concerned," he
said. "Just how many of these here fair fights have
you been in? Must be a dozen or more by now."

Magatagan, arms folded across his chest, consid-

6

ered the marshal quietly. Anger was stirring through him, and standing out in the hot, driving sunlight served only to add to his rising temper. The question, too, with its snide inference, was a further irritant.

"I hear tell it's twice that," he said dryly. "Some folks claim it's more."

"Maybe," the lawman countered. "Your story'd be a mite different anyway. What'd you have against Nat Locklear?"

"His name's Bigbee, not Locklear. Family matter. Goes back a spell."

"I'd like to hear about it—"

Magatagan's reply was firm, flat. "No point—just take my word for it, Marshal. Bigbee got what he had coming to him."

"Your word—that sure ain't much for me to go on."

"Expect you'll find out it's good no matter what you think. Now, am I going to have trouble with you or can I ride on?"

The marshal glanced about at the crowd. He shrugged. "I ain't stopping you. Locklear had a gun, was trying to use it. Law says it's self-defense at a time like that for either man—which lets you off the hook. But the way I see it Nat Locklear was like all them other hard-luck fellows you've buried—they just wasn't fast enough with their gun."

"Whatever you say, Marshal," Magatagan murmured, and continued on to his waiting horse.

Reaching the rack fronting the Yellow Jacket, Reno checked the cinch of the saddle on the bay horse he was riding, and finding it to his satisfaction, he swung up onto the big gelding, cut back to the center of the street, and headed south. He drew abreast the marshal and the dozen or so men gathered about the lawman, and looking neither to the right nor to the left, rode on by, a curious sort of tension having its way with him. It was a feeling born not of fear, but of uncertainty; he could not recall ever being permitted by a lawman to ride on so quickly after a shoot-out as he was by the marshal of Las Vegas.

Ordinarily it meant at least a day or two in a jail if on nothing more than general principles, and as he moved by the tall lawman, he half-expected the man to sing out and order him to halt. But no such command came and Magatagan pressed on.

Reaching the lower limits of the settlement, Reno paused and glanced back over his shoulder. No one was following, and that, too, seemed a bit odd. All too many times during the years, he had ridden out of a town with a posse or a vengeful relative hot on his trail.

Magatagan sighed, settled comfortably in his saddle, and put the bay into an easy lope. The law was not through with him, he knew—nor would it ever be. The search for Henry Bigbee was over, and the vow he'd made to his mother was settled—but he'd made too many mistakes along the way, and those were far from satisfied. Likely they never would be, until the lawmen still looking for him caught up and took him back to face the charges lodged against him.

Mostly such resulted from shoot-outs—men he had encountered in the long hunt for Bigbee, during which he had grown from a man good with a pistol to one so expert that many felt tempted to try their luck at matching his talent.

And there were those times when his poke was

near empty, and offers were made by men needing a job done to hire him and his gun. It was always easy money, and he never questioned the right or the wrong of it, simply did what he was being paid to do—and ridden on, several hundred dollars better off.

But that, too, was behind him now, just as was the long search for Henry Bigbee, who had been made to pay for what he had done. Again a hard, rueful smile parted Reno Magatagan's lips; it was all over, yes, but he had turned himself into a wanted outlaw—a feared killer that a dozen lawmen in an equal number of towns scattered throughout the west would give a year's pay to apprehend.

Drawing his sack of tobacco and a fold of thin, brown papers from a vest pocket, Reno rolled a cigarette, lit it with a match fired by a thumbnail, and settled deeper into his saddle.

What came next? He had been virtually unknown in New Mexico Territory, but that would change now. Eventually the word of his killing Henry Bigbee would reach lawmen elsewhere who were looking for him, and shortly thereafter they would be riding the hills and flats and poking about the towns endeavoring to locate him.

He grinned once again as a thought came to him. The marshal of Las Vegas, who evidently had only a passing acquaintance with his reputation and had been made aware of his identity only that morning by someone local recognizing him, would be in for some hard words from outside lawmen when they learned of the Bigbee shoot-out. He should have jailed the killer, the marshal would be told; he had a wanted man in his hands and had let him go.

But the lawman should not be blamed too much. Las Vegas was a long way from Missouri, Kansas, Nebraska, and other points north, and communication being practically nonexistent, like as not the marshal had no idea at all that his visitor, there so briefly, was a much-sought-after outlaw.

Mexico. Magatagan reckoned that was his best bet. He could go there, lie low for a year or two until he figured he was forgotten, and then return, head for California or Oregon. He wasn't too well-heeled as far as cash went, having maybe a couple of hundred dollars between his pockets and his money belt, but he reckoned he could find some kind of a job once he got to a place where he could quit looking over his shoulder.

Being a cowhand had never appealed to him, but he supposed he could learn. What would be more suited to his talents would be a guard at a silver or gold mine, or maybe riding shotgun on an ore wagon. Mining was booming in Mexico, he'd heard, and the chances for getting on a mine payroll should be good.

If he could land himself a job at decent pay, he ought to be able to save most of what he earned. Then, when he felt it was safe to pull out, he'd have a pretty good stake, one that would allow him to buy land in California, or maybe Oregon, and settle down.

Reno liked the thought of that: a place of his own, a few cows and horses, a garden where things could grow, and who could say, perhaps a wife and children, a family of his own someday? It wasn't far-fetched; it was entirely possible, in fact, if he could stay out of reach of the past until he became a forgotten man.

The elation of such glowing prospects ended abruptly. A wariness born of years of experience prompted Magatagan to again glance over his shoulder. At once a hardness came into his eyes. He'd thought no one was on his trail, but there was: a lone rider bent low over his saddle and coming on fast.

A lawman from Kansas? From Nebraska, or Missouri, or could it be a federal marshal from the Indian Territory? It would be difficult to tell without a face-to-face meeting—not that identity in such instances meant anything: The law was his enemy; it mattered little where it hailed from.

True, it could be just some cowhand or pilgrim on his way to a distant town, and in a hurry to get there. Reno shook off that possibility, an inner comprehension telling him that such was not likely, that the rider was probably a lawman who just happened into Las Vegas shortly after the shoot-out and was giving chase or some member of Bigbee's family out to take vengeance. At any rate it was a matter to be dealt with quickly.

Magatagan glanced about. He saw that he was in fairly open country, that the mighty Sangre de Cristo Mountains were well to the west, too far to reach without being seen by the fast-approaching rider.

He could of course simply halt, take up a stand behind one of the thick squat juniper trees that dotted the countryside, confront the rider when he drew near, and use his gun, thus putting an end to being followed.

That solution, however, did not appeal to Magata-

gan. He'd like to think that the shooting of Henry
Bigbee was his last, that he would never again use
the .44 hanging at his side unless forced to do so in
defense of his life.

That hope could end soon, Reno realized, unless
he took measures to avoid a meeting. Again he looked
about. A dozen or so yards ahead, a trail cut off
toward the mountains. It ran on in sight for a distance, was finally lost in a maze of tall brush, rocks,
and trees extending, fingerlike, from the foot of the
towering hills.

Reno spurred forward at once, turned onto the
trail, taking care as he did to leave a clear trail in the
event the rider did not note his turning off, and
hurried on to the trees. Once there, he pulled back
into the dark shadows and, well concealed by brush,
waited.

If the rider was not in pursuit of him, odds were he'd
continue on down the road that led to Santa Fe and
other points south; if he was, then very shortly the
rider would be moving past the pocket of under-
growth and trees and he would know who it was that
was following him.

The rapid hammer of the horse's hooves began to
fill the air, first as faint, hollow-sounding, rhythmic
taps, and then louder, more pronounced thuds.
Magatagan, still in the saddle, kept his eyes on the
road. The rider surged into view, slowed, halted at
the turnoff. After several moments he dismounted
and examined the ground more closely. Abruptly he
rose, climbed back into his saddle, and turned onto
the trail leading to the mountains.

Reno swore deeply. There could be no doubt; the
rider was trailing him. But who was he? Twice
Magatagan had gotten a fairly clear look at the man's

face and found no recognition. Was he a bounty hunter working on one of the numerous posters that had been issued offering a substantial reward for him, or was it as he'd earlier thought it might be—a relative of Henry Bigbee out to even the score?

Magatagan glanced down to his side. His hand, unbidden, had dropped to the pistol holstered there. Another survival instinct from the past, he thought, and drawing his arm back, he allowed his fingers to grip the horn of the saddle while he put his attention once more on the rider.

He was no lawman that he knew. Magatagan saw moments later that probably he was not a lawman at all since he was not wearing a badge. And the man—young, now sitting straight on the sorrel he was riding, rifle across his lap—did not have the looks of a bounty hunter. As he drew abreast, his eyes moved neither right nor left but maintained a straight-ahead direction, apparently convinced that the man he was trailing was still in front of him.

Magatagan waited out a full quarter-hour, wanting to make certain the rider, whoever he was, did not alter course and backtrack, and then, when there was no indication of such, he rode out of the brush pocket and, still keeping to the trees, resumed the road south. Reno hoped he'd seen the last of the mysterious rider, but there was no guarantee of such; if the man seriously wanted to overtake him, he would simply double back once he realized he was headed wrong and would pick up the bay gelding's trail once more.

But by then he would be well down the trail, Magatagan thought with satisfaction; too, the oncoming of darkness would increase his chances for not seeing the rider on the sorrel again.

Reno rode on, coming, near the end of the day, to a point where the Sangre de Cristos had fallen behind him and only plains and low, rolling hills country lay around him. He had caught no further signs of the man on the sorrel, but an inner caution kept Reno in the saddle, and he kept moving until well after night had fallen before halting to make camp.

He was up before first light, breakfasted on coffee, hard tack, and dried meat, and pushed on. Around midmorning he came to a fork in the trail; a sun-faded sign on the left-hand branch, pointing east, said: TASCOSA: the one on the right stated SOCORRO. He hadn't planned on getting as far west as the latter settlement, but he reckoned it really didn't matter too much, it being in the general direction he was going, and since he'd seen nothing of the rifleman on the sorrel, he swung off the due-south course he was following—one that would take him onto endless plains country—and struck for a range of mountains looming up well in the distance.

Near noon of the next day he reached them, passing near but not through several small Mexican settlements en route. A cut that appeared to be much used by wagons and other travelers allowed him to cross through the mountain range to its western side, where he had a glimpse of a fairly wide river winding like a silver ribbon along the bottom of a lush, green valley. The Rio Grande, Reno assumed, and nodded in satisfaction. It was the same as a well-marked road leading south to Mexico.

He followed the river closely, camping at night on its grassy banks and enjoying the shade of the giant cottonwoods, plentiful everywhere, during the days. Forsaking his usual custom of avoiding settlements, he paused at several, at some to replenish his stock of trail grub and buy a bit of grain for the bay, at others just to treat himself to a drink.

Reno spent two days and nights in the town called Socorro, a place that marked the northern end of a trail coming up from Mexico that was called the Jornada del Muerto, which, one of the Mexican saloon girls told him, meant Journey of the Dead Man.

He might have considered staying longer in Socorro, had the recollection of the man on the sorrel, and the probability that he was still following, not come to mind. His own safety, at least from the law, lay across the border, and while the rifleman on the sorrel would not likely be deterred by that, he could be dealt with if he persisted.

Magatagan rode on the morning of the third day, angling away from the river and bearing more to the west. Nogales, a town just across the border separating Mexico from the Civil War-born territory of Arizona, offered good possibilities for work, he'd been told, and changing his loosely prepared original plan, Reno now pointed for it.

As he worked steadily south and west, Magatagan had noticed the increase in the heat. He learned one day from a passing drummer moving north with his wagonload of tinware and other household items, that he was heading into the great Sonoran Desert, and he'd best get used to extreme heat. Reno shrugged off the suggestion. He was enjoying the weather— clear and hot under a spotless blue sky during the daylight hours, cool and comfortable at night.

He should be getting near Mexico, Magatagan figured several days later, and then on the afternoon following that wishful thought, he spotted smoke hanging on the horizon and reckoned he was almost there. But it proved otherwise.

It turned out to be a town—either in New Mexico or in Arizona, he was not sure which—that, he learned later, straddled an old stagecoach route to California, one that had been abandoned for a shorter road. LYNCHBURG, the sign at the end of the dusty main street proclaimed, and standing near it was another, pointing to the south and bearing the words: MEXICO 20 MILES.

Magatagan guessed he was close enough to his goal to lay over for a day or two, wash the dust from his throat, and let the bay rest while he saw what he could find out about work on the other side of the border. Raking the gelding with his spurs, he continued on into the center of the road, somewhat surprised at the lack of persons along the board sidewalks, and he slanted for one of the larger structures bearing across its front in bold black letters:

BULL'S HEAD SALOON

LIQUOR . . . WOMEN . . . GAMBLING . . . DANCING . . .

That was exactly the place he was looking for, Reno had decided.

☆ **4** ☆

Stabling the weary bay in the barn at the rear of the Bull's Head and giving instructions as to his care, Magatagan returned to the street and, mounting the wide porch fronting the saloon, entered through its open doorway.

The immediate greeting of smoke, liquor smells, music, and steady rumble of conversation punctuated by laughter was welcome . . . and familiar. On the move for the past ten years or so, Reno had spent a great deal of that time, when not riding, in the saloons, enjoying himself while he asked the questions that eventually led him to Henry Bigbee. Thus the noisy confusion was something akin to a homecoming.

Although it was still three or four hours until dark, the Bull's Head was well-patronized. At least three dozen or more men were in the large square room, some at the lengthy, ornate bar, a few trying their luck at the poker and blackjack tables or the chuck-a-luck cage.

Three couples were on the small, cleared area reserved for dancing, each stomping out a clog to the tune of "Buffalo Girl" being pounded out by a heavyset woman at a piano. Two gaudily dressed girls were posing at the foot of a staircase that led up to a second floor. Beyond an upper railing Reno

18

could see a hallway with doors that turned off into rooms where the women plied their trade.

Glancing back over his shoulder to the slowly darkening street, and seeing no one, Magatagan crossed to an open space at the end of the counter and beckoned to the bartender—a dour-faced man with a waxed, handlebar mustache.

"Whiskey—"

The barman nodded, produced a glass, and filled it almost to the rim from a near-full bottle.

"That'll be two-bits," he said.

Reno dropped a silver dollar on the bar, collected his change, and taking up his drink, turned to observe the activities taking place around him. He was hungry, he realized, but pushed the need aside for the time being; he'd rustle up a meal later. Right now it was good just to have a couple of drinks and relieve the trail weariness—and loneliness—that always seemed to grip him at the end of the day.

Tossing off the initial portion of liquor, Magatagan turned back to the bar and, pushing his empty glass toward the center of the counter, laid another quarter beside it. The bartender saw the move, and immediately producing a bottle, he refilled the small container.

"Any place around close where a man can get a bite to eat?" Reno asked, wrapping his fingers around the glass.

"Sure—right here," the bartender replied. "Special today's boiled beans and ham. Or you can get yourself steak and fried spuds."

"I'll go with the steak," Magatagan said.

"You be wanting coffee, too?"

"Can forget the java—I'll stick with whiskey and a pitcher of water."

The barkeeper nodded, pointed to several empty

tables and chairs in the back of the room. "Pick yourself out a place to set. I'll have one of the girls bring your grub."

Magatagan took up his drink, the liquor slowly dispelling the fatigue that dragged at him, and turned toward the rear of the saloon. Abruptly the back door flung open. A squat, thick-shouldered man entered, struggling with the slight figure of a girl. He had the youngster—dark-haired, eyes wide with fear—around the waist with one muscular arm, while the hand of the other was clamped over her mouth, stifling her cries.

Once inside, the stocky man took a firmer grip on the girl, kicked the door shut with a heel, and turned to face a well-dressed man who had emerged from a room off to the side not visible to Magatagan.

"Got a humdinger here!" the husky man said, arms tightening about the struggling girl. "Them soldier boys'll pay a month's wages to crawl in bed with her!"

The well-dressed man, apparently the owner of the Bull's Head, nodded approvingly. He reminded Reno of a gambler he'd known down New Orleans way— sleek, dark, sly, almost womanlike . . . but deadly as a cocked six-gun.

"Who is she?" Magatagan heard him ask.

"Hell, I don't know, Rand!" the tough replied, struggling with the girl. "And who cares? Lives around here somewheres, I reckon. Seen her walking down the alley behind the hotel and grabbed her. Don't matter none, does it? Or are you getting choosy?"

"Don't make a damn to me," Rand snapped.

"Was just wondering." He and the man with the girl were not visible to the saloon's patrons because of the arrangement of the bar, which ran almost the full width of the room, but from where Reno was standing at the end of the counter, they were in full view.

"You're getting mighty touchy lately, Jed! I'm just wanting to be sure we ain't got hold of somebody's kid who might put up a stink."

"Ain't likely," the man called Jed answered, savagely jerking the girl about. "She's prob'ly one of them trail orphans living with some family that'll be glad to get shed of her."

Magatagan listened with no particular interest. It was a rule of his to never interfere in something that was none of his business, and while the methods of the Bull's Head owner in recruiting girls for his upstairs brothel was a bit high-handed, there was nothing new to it. Bawdy houses throughout the frontier were populated by unwilling as well as willing women.

"Well, get her upstairs by the back way and lock her in one of the storage rooms," Rand directed. "I'll look in on her after a bit."

Magatagan frowned. The girl was looking directly at him, eyes wide with fright and filled with frantic appeal. That she was a trail orphan—an unfortunate child left without kin by an Indian attack or fatal accident of some sort, and living on the suffrage of some family—seemed unlikely to him. The dress and shoes she was wearing and her overall appearance did not indicate the semislavery conditions that usually befell those consigned to such a life.

"H-help me please!"

The girl had managed to wrench free of the hand crushing her mouth and gasped out a plea for aid.

Jed slapped her viciously, cut off any more words

with his thick hand. The girl continued to struggle, her eyes never leaving Reno.

This was one time he'd have to break his rule of keeping out of something that did not pertain to him, Magatagan decided suddenly. Setting his empty glass on the bar, he crossed quickly to where Jed was holding the girl.

"Turn her loose," he directed, halting in front of the squat man, and then, not waiting for the man to comply willingly—which Reno knew he would not—he drew his pistol and clubbed the burly man solidly alongside his head.

As Jed stumbled back, Magatagan reached for the girl, drew her in behind him. In that same moment Rand hurriedly wheeled and ducked into a room, evidently his office, a few steps away, and closed the door.

"Damn you—butting in!" Jed's voice caught Magatagan's attention. "I'll learn you to go—"

The squat man's words broke off as he gathered himself and, crouched low, charged. Magatagan, cursing softly, pushed the girl more to one side. Continuing to observe another rule of long standing that he'd followed faithfully through the years—that of always protecting his gun hand—he grasped more firmly the heavy .44 he was holding and prepared to use it as a club again.

☆ **5** ☆

Mouthing curses, Jed rushed in, big, knotted fists swinging. Someone in front of the bar, either hearing the sounds of what was taking place or catching a glimpse of Magatagan's tense, poised figure, let out a yell.

"Fight! There's a fight back there!"

As the entire patronage and hired help of the Bull's Head gravitated toward the rear of the saloon for a closer look, Reno stepped lightly away, avoiding Jed's headlong charge. The stocky man caught himself, wheeled amazingly fast, and surged back. This time Magatagan did not give way. Bringing up an arm, he laid a solid blow again on the husky man's temple with the heavy .44. The sound of it was a meaty thud that could be heard throughout the saloon. Jed halted in stride, spun about, and collapsed in a heap.

A round of cheers and a few disapproving catcalls filled the smoky interior of the Bull's Head. One of the soldiers Reno had noticed earlier at the bar pushed his way through the crowd and knelt beside the senseless man. He glanced up at Magatagan.

"Why don't you use your fists instead of that there damn gun?" he demanded.

Reno smiled slightly as he holstered the weapon.

23

"You fight your way—I'll fight mine," he replied, and turning away, he put his attention on the girl. Young, pretty, she could be no more than fifteen or sixteen, he was certain.

"I-I want to thank you," she managed, her words barely audible above the clamor of conversation going on about them.

He had been right, Magatagan saw, to interfere. The girl was not the sort cut out for a life in a bawdy house. "Was pleased to help."

"My name's Abby Roth," the girl volunteered. Her eyes were red from tears, and there were dark bruises on her arms where Jed's brutal fingers had left their mark. "My mother has the dressmaking shop down the street."

"Best you get there fast," Magatagan said, stepping aside so that the bartender and another man could carry the still-unconscious Jed toward Rand's office. "And you mind where and when you do your walking. Next time there might not be somebody around to help you."

Abby nodded. "I'd just delivered a dress for my mother and was on my way home. It's always risky to be out after dark—I know that—but it couldn't be helped this time." She paused, her eyes on the men disappearing into the owner of the Bull's Head's office. "I-I was so scared when that man, Jed, stepped out of a doorway and grabbed me that I couldn't make a sound. And then, when he brought me here—"

"He ever bother you before?"

Abby, continuing to dab at her eyes, shook her head. "I've seen him watching me, but that's all."

"Thing for you to do is be more careful from here on in," Reno said. "You want me to walk you home?"

"No, I'll be all right. I can keep to the middle of the street," the girl said, turning toward the door at the rear of the saloon. "Thank you again."

Magatagan watched her disappear into the night and then, coming about, resumed his place at the bar. Ignoring the glances turned on him—some friendly, some puzzled, others frankly hostile—he beckoned to the bartender for another drink. As the man filled a clean glass, Reno handed over the necessary coin and then pointed to a nearby table.

"I'll take my supper now," he said. "You'll find me sitting there."

The barkeep, features expressionless, inclined his head slightly and moved away. The fight would have been no more than a minor incident in the man's daily routine, Reno knew. Brawls were common in any saloon.

Taking up his glass of whiskey, Magatagan stepped away from the counter and, crossing to the table he'd indicated, sat down on one of the hard, straight-back chairs. Activities in the Bull's Head were in full swing again. The smoke coils hanging around the oil chandeliers had thickened, the piano player was again pounding out a dance melody for a handful of couples, and the line at the bar had increased. More men were to be seen in the casino area, where shouts erupted regularly when a player enjoyed a bit of good fortune.

Traffic on the stairs leading to the second floor was steady, and there were now no women standing idly about at the railing of the balcony and there were but a few wandering through the crowd. Here and there Magatagan spotted soldiers, and recalling what Jed had said to Rand about the profit possibilities of

Abby, Reno guessed there was an army camp or fort somewhere nearby.

A fight broke out between two men on the far side of the room, apparently over the attentions of one of the gayly dressed girls, who was now standing back, looking on. The bartender, craning his neck to see as he sought to assess the seriousness of the altercation, turned to a burly individual standing behind the counter, muscular arms folded over a thick chest.

"Better get over there and stop that, Charlie," Magatagan heard him say. "They're liable to bust up the place—and Jed ain't going to be around to look after things."

The burly man moved off into the crowd and pushed his way to where the contestants, now locked in each other's arms, were wrestling back and forth. They broke apart immediately when Charlie caught them by their shoulders. Giving each a shove, he sent them reeling back into nearby chairs. At that point the circle of onlookers began to break up, and Charlie, making his way back through the customers, resumed his place behind the bar.

"Was that damned Cherry again," he said, reporting to the bartender. "She ain't nothing but trouble. The boss sure ought to get rid of her."

Once again the saloon settled down to its normal bustling pace. Two men at the bar got into a loud argument over the war, now long past, and for a few minutes it appeared as if another fight would get underway as barely scabbed-over wounds were raked open once more by words being said.

Fortunately friends of the pair took a hand, and both were quickly hustled off—one being taken into the casino, the other propelled over to the piano, where he was taken charge of by one of the girls who led him out onto the dance floor, there to join the half-dozen or so other couples stomping and whirling about to the almost inaudible music.

At that moment Magatagan saw his evening meal coming toward him on a tray carried by a girl, attractive despite the heavy coating of rouge and powder on her face. She approached the table smiling, brown eyes bright, hair pulled to the nape of her neck, arching breasts visible above the low, circular collar of the bright-red dress she was wearing.

"I'm Dolly Jo," she stated, placed the tray before him. "You want company while you eat?"

Magatagan grinned. "Sure. Fetch us a bottle from the bartender, a glass for yourself—and sit down."

Dolly Jo dropped back to the bar, returned quickly with a full quart of whiskey and the glass. Seating herself on one of the chairs, she uncorked the liquor, filled his empty glass and then her own.

"I'm wanting to thank you—me and all the girls—for what you done," she said.

Magatagan, slicing into the thick steak on his tin plate, looked up, frowned.

"Jed—Jed Bleeker," the girl explained, seeing his puzzled expression. "We've been hoping and praying somebody'd come along and give him a beating." Dolly Jo hesitated and glanced about. Lowering her voice, she added, "Wouldn't have been nobody sorry around this town if you'd blowed his damned head off!"

Magatagan resumed eating. Then, "He done that before? Dragged in some girl off the street so's she'd work here, I mean?"

Dolly Jo sipped at her whiskey. "Once or twice that I recall. Never did try it with a kid like that one, though. You know, it's kind of awkward, us a-talking and me not knowing who I'm talking to. Mind telling me your name?''

"Magatagan—"

Dolly Jo smiled. "That all there is to it?"

"All anybody needs to know," he said, "but if it matters all that much to you, the first part is Reno."

"Reno Magatagan," Dolly Jo repeated as if enjoying the sound of it. "Rest of mine's Morrison—Dolly Jo Morrison."

"Right pretty name—fits," Magatagan said. "Was a gambler-looking jasper that come out of a room in the back. This Jed called him Rand. He the owner?"

Dolly Jo nodded. "Yeh, Monroe Rand. Most folks call him Monty. Heard from somebody that he once was only a gambler here, then ended up owning the place. Don't know just exactly how it happened."

Magatagan, enjoying the meat and potatoes, smiled. "A gambler with the touch can sure surprise. Usually got more tricks up their sleeves than a horse has hairs."

Dolly Jo had emptied her glass, was refilling it. "You aim to hang around here long?"

"Not sure. Sort of passing through—"

"On your way to Mexico," the girl finished.

Reno looked up. "Now, what makes you say that?"

Dolly Jo's shoulders stirred under the thin fabric of her red dress. "Most men just riding through—and with the look I see in your eyes—are headed for the border."

"Running from the law, you mean?"

"Yeh, or from some other man. But you don't look like the kind that'd run from anybody."

Magatagan grinned, laid down his knife and fork, the plate now clean. "Fact is, I am," he said, thinking of the rider on the sorrel—a relative of Henry

Bigbee's, he had finally concluded. "Leastwise I figure I am."

Dolly Jo refilled his near-empty glass with whiskey. He shook his head, returned the liquor to the bottle, and poured himself a glass of water from the pitcher and downed it.

"You think you might be? I don't understand—" the girl said, puzzled.

"Saw a man on my trail coming on fast. Turned off into some brush to see if he was tracking me or just headed in the same direction. Happened he turned off, too."

"You didn't know him?"

"Nope, was a stranger, but I sort of got a hunch he's related to a man I had to settle a score with."

"But you're not sure—" Dolly Jo began, and then broke off as she saw a distinct change come over Magatagan's strong features.

"Move back—away from the table," he murmured, eyes on two men moving slowly toward them. "Looks like a mite of trouble coming."

☆ **6** ☆

Dolly Jo pushed her chair back carefully. "Who are they?" she asked, sliding a glance at the approaching riders.

"The Converses. Tall one's called Duke. Other one's named Abel. Had a run-in with their older brother, Ike. Ended up with him being dead. They swore they'd get even someday. I reckon they're figuring that time has come."

A sort of excitement had claimed Reno Magatagan, filling his eyes, tightening the planes of his face, and turning his mouth into a grim, down-curving line. It was as if the possibility of trouble was welcome, as if he looked forward to the violence it would bring. Easing back in his chair, he let his hands sink to his sides.

The Converse brothers—hard-bitten, bearded, rough-looking men—came to a halt two or three strides from where Reno sat. Patrons behind them in the saloon, instantly sensing what was to come, hurriedly removed themselves from the line of fire while a heavy silence again fell over the saloon.

Duke Converse, hands behind his back, smiled tightly. "Been hoping to see you again, killer—"

"That so?" Magatagan said quietly.

Abel had his hands out of sight also, and both of

their holsters were empty, which meant, simply, they had already drawn their guns and were holding them ready for instant use. Reno smiled crookedly at the subterfuge.

"Surprised we ain't met before. I get around pretty much—"

"Yeh," Duke said, "seems you do."

Magatagan raised his left arm slowly, brushed his hat to the back of his head. "What's on your mind?"

"Same thing there was the day you shot down Ike," Duke yelled, and brought his gun about fast.

Magatagan, anticipating the instant, rocked to one side. He triggered his pistol from under the table, saw Duke flinch as the bullet tore into him. Abel fired in almost the same moment. Reno felt the slug sear across his upper arm as he got off a second shot into Abel Converse.

Magatagan was motionless for several long moments and then rose to his feet. Powder smoke was drifting upward from him, and the sharp, biting odor of it touched everyone nearby. The hush in the Bull's Head hung for a long, breathless minute, and then broke as a gust of voices broke out.

Reno, wise to the ways of men at such times, pointed his weapon at the floor and drove a third bullet into the wooden planking to command attention. The law would come now, and he wanted it made clear by all in the saloon that the shoot-out had been forced upon him by the Converse brothers.

"You all seen what happened," he called in a voice that reached every corner of the Bull's Head. "Gunplay was not my idea. Had to do what I done or get killed myself."

There was no immediate response as Magatagan glanced about. The bartender, he noted, was talking to Charlie, the burly man who had broken up the fight on the far side of the room. Whatever was said, Charlie was not in agreement as he shook his head not once but several times.

"There anybody in here faulting what I said?" Reno pressed.

"You're damn right—was them two that crowded you into using your gun," a voice responded quickly. Immediately others took it up.

"Both of them had their irons out, was all set to cut you down. Hell, they wasn't aiming to give you a chance!"

"The tall one there—was him that shot first—"

Magatagan, satisfied, flipped open the loading gate of the .44, rodded out the spent cartridges, and thumbed in fresh ones. Then, as Charlie, with the aid of several bystanders, began to drag the Converse brothers off toward the back door, he settled again onto his chair.

Dolly Jo, her eyes glowing, resumed her place at the table. Quickly filling his empty glass from the bottle of whiskey, she pushed it toward him, smiling tightly.

"You knew all the time what they aimed to do—and you outsmarted them, shot them before they—"

The girl broke off abruptly, glance on the spreading bloodstain on his sleeve. "You've been hit! I didn't know—"

"Creased me, that's all," Reno said, downing the liquor.

"But you're bleeding—the flesh could mortify if you don't take care of it!" Dolly Jo protested. "We'll go up to my room and I'll take care of it."

Magatagan stared moodily into his empty glass and

shook his head. "Maybe later. Best I wait here until the law shows up and I get things straightened out."

"Law!" she echoed. "There ain't no law here in this town—leastwise not the kind you're talking about."

Magatagan's lips pulled into a hard smile. "Well, now, that's a right nice thing to hear. Ain't there anybody that keeps things going straight?"

"In here. Jed Bleeker, the man you knocked out, and Charlie Mason—he's the big one standing behind the bar with Pete—they look after the saloon. That's what Rand pays them to do."

"Sounds like Rand's sort of the high card around here."

"He's wanting to be, but there's still enough towns-people around to keep him from taking over—them and the army."

"Spotted a few soldiers in the crowd. And Bleeker was telling Rand that they'd make a pile of money off them with that girl he dragged in—"

Dolly Jo fingered her glass of liquor and stared unseeingly at the shifting, noisy crowd in the saloon.

"That'd be what they'd see in her, all right—just a lot of money. She's lucky you stepped in."

"The army a big thing around here?"

"Guess you could say so—fort's not far. They make things pretty bad for regular folks."

"Expect that's why I didn't see anybody on the street when I rode in."

"Probably. A lot of them come in late in the day, and folks've learned it's best to stay out of sight until they've holed up somewhere or gone back to the fort."

"You have any trouble with them?"

"No, not especially. A girl learns to get along

with them and every other man that comes along, else Jed Bleeker will teach her a thing or two—and he does his teaching with his fists."

"Looks to be the kind, all right. You ever have any problem with him?"

"Only once—right after I came here. My husband got himself killed on a cattle drive, left me with nothing. A woman broke and alone in this country don't have much choice when it comes to staying alive. What few jobs there are, the local ones already have, so it's a saloon or starve, and men figure a woman working in one's there for just one thing, to satisfy them."

"Guess that's how it's always been."

"And always will be," Dolly Jo added wearily. "You want to go upstairs with me now?"

Magatagan nodded. "Take the bottle along," he said, and rising, he crossed to the bar. Conversation ceased abruptly as the bartender, Pete, hurried up to face him.

"What do I owe you?" Reno asked.

Pete glanced to the table. "Grub, quart of our best liquor—five dollars'll cover it all."

Magatagan laid the necessary amount on the bar and started to turn away. He paused as Pete's voice reached him.

"You figure to be around much longer, Mister—Mister—"

"Hard to say," Magatagan replied, ignoring the man's obvious attempt to learn his name. "Can tell you more about it in a couple of days," he finished, and moving on, he followed Dolly Jo up the stairs to her quarters.

Dolly Jo's room proved to be small, providing space enough for a bed, stove, chair, washstand, and a curtained wardrobe. To relieve its barrenness the woman had hung a half-dozen or so pictures cut from magazines and calendars on the plank walls. There was no carpet on the floor, and light was supplied by a single lamp.

"Welcome to my home," Dolly Jo said in a flippant attempt at humor. "Not much, but it serves its purpose . . . Take off your shirt. I'll wash it after I've seen to that wound."

Magatagan removed his gun belt, hung it on a bedpost, followed that with his vest and shirt. That done, he sank into the rocking chair, treated himself to a drink, and then placed the bottle of whiskey on the floor nearby.

"Just can't savvy how a town this size can get by without a lawman," he said as Dolly Jo, a pan of water and a fold of white cloth in her hands, crouched beside him and began to cleanse the shallow groove Abel Converse's bullet had left in his arm.

"It would be a hard job," the woman said, and paused. "You ain't thinking about taking it, are you?"

Reno laughed. "Hell, no! Just that I can't recollect

ever being in a town, big or little, that didn't have a lawman of some kind. There some reason for it?''

Dolly Jo, satisfied with the cleaning, reached for the bottle of whiskey. Taking another bit of cloth, she folded it into a pad, soaked it thoroughly with the liquor, and pressed it against the wound.

Magatagan cursed as the alcohol bit into the raw flesh, eased the pain with another long swallow from the bottle. By then Dolly Jo had prepared another strip of cloth, and keeping the compress firmly against the wound, she wrapped the bandage about his arm and tied it securely.

''That ought to do it,'' she murmured, returning the pan to the stove and placing the remainder of the cloth on a shelf. Taking his shirt, she put it in the china bowl on the washstand and poured a quantity of water from the pitcher over it.

''Best to let it soak a bit before I wash it out,'' she explained, sitting down on the edge of the bed. Then, picking up the conversation, she said, ''You keep wondering about why the town doesn't have a lawman. Expect it did, years ago, but after the stage quit coming through, the place sort of died off and a lot of folks moved away.

''Ever since—like I said—it's been sort of a fight between Monty Rand, the people still here, and the army over who's going to run things.''

''Can't see that the army's got any business horning in—''

''That's a big argument, too. I'm not too sure about some of the details—I've just heard it talked around—but a man named Lynch who homesteaded here a long time back built his place on what he thought was open land. Later on, when folks started moving west, his house became a stopover for water and other things. Lynch turned his house into a regular store, and after that, it all grew into a town that got pretty big when the California stagecoaches started running through.

"Nobody found out about the town being on government property until the war started and they decided to build a fort. It was the surveyors that came up with the news that the town was in the wrong place and had to move. People here didn't pay any attention to the order. They had built homes here, and merchants had their stores and such. Anyway, Lynch had homestead papers to prove he was in the right. So nothing happened. Folks just set tight, and the thing kind of wound down into this three-way squabble that's going on now."

It was hot in the room. Dolly Jo brushed at the shine on her cheeks, shrugged. "Heard a couple of weeks ago that the colonel out at the fort had gone back to Washington to straighten out the mixup—if he could. Maybe when he gets back we'll all know what's what."

"How far's the fort from here?"

The woman's shoulders stirred, and reaching for the bottle, she had a small drink. "Eight or ten miles. Don't exactly know."

"Close enough anyway to make the soldiers pretty regular customers—"

"For certain. And they pay cash, something Monty likes."

Dolly Jo lay back on the bed. The dull thump of the couples dancing, the faint notes of the piano mingling with the drone of voices were barely audible in the night.

"Heard Pete ask you how long you aimed to be

around," she said. "You changed your mind any—
or you still just passing through?"

"Can't see as there's any reason to stick around.
Besides, I've got that fellow with a rifle looking for
me—and there's the Converse boys now. No doubt
they've got friends who'll get some ideas."

"I doubt if they or anybody else would scare you
off, unless you just wanted it that way."

"You're right there. It's just that I'm trying to
dodge any more shootings. Back up the trail a piece I
done what I started out to do about ten years ago—
track down and kill the man who let my pa die. Was
a vow I made to my ma. Guess you could say it was
sort of a family thing. I found him, done what I had
to, and then told myself he was the last man I'd ever
kill. The Converses changed that right quick."

"You didn't have a choice. Anyway, you could
start with them."

"I reckon I can, but I'm wondering if I can keep
that promise to myself. Was hoping to go down into
Mexico where nobody'll know me—and the lawmen
who're still looking for me can't follow—and start
over. Then, someday, when everything's blown over,
come back, maybe settle in Oregon or California."

Dolly Jo, face turned to Reno as she lay on the
bed, studied him thoughtfully. "I can't count the
number of times I've heard a man say that same
thing. Do you really think you can ever put away
your gun?"

"Like a mule, I can't do nothing but try, and—"

A sudden, insistent pounding on the door broke
into Reno Magatagan's words. Instinctively he leaned
forward and quickly lifted his pistol from its holster.
Dolly Jo smiled sympathetically, knowing that for
him it would always be that way, and shook her

head. Rising, she crossed to the door and opened it a crack. A man's deep voice, slurred and demanding, filled the small room. Magatagan got to his feet at once and stepped up beside the woman.

"You looking for somebody?" he asked, his question sharp.

The cowhand's mouth gaped. He took a step backward as his eyes widened. "No, sir—I sure ain't!" he mumbled, and wheeling, headed back up the hall.

Dolly Jo laughed as she closed and locked the door. "He's an old friend," she explained, returning to the bed. "I guess seeing you here scared him pretty bad. . . . You figure to spend the night with me?"

"Only about half of it," Magatagan said, moving toward her. "Wouldn't be fair to your regular customers was I to do that."

☆ 8 ☆

Lucilla Roth paused at the parlor window of her house and glanced toward the street. A worried frown drew her brows together. It was getting dark; Abby should have returned from the errand she'd sent her on by now. Lucilla wished she'd waited until morning to deliver the dress, but Mrs. Willcox had insisted on having it that night—and Edith Willcox was one of her best customers.

It did no good to worry, she reminded herself. She'd give Abby ten more minutes, then go and look for her. It could be the girl had stopped to talk with a friend, or perhaps Edith Willcox had insisted she stay for tea and cookies. Likely that was it: Abby was still at Mrs. Willcox's.

Turning, Lucilla moved back into the center of the room, neat and cozy with its faded, flowered rug, lace curtains, sturdy furniture complemented with crocheted antimicassars, family pictures on the papered walls, and a large lamp set squarely in the center of the library table.

The furnishings in the parlor, along with all the rest in the small house built behind the dressmaking shop, had come west with them—her husband, Will, their daughter, Abby, and of course, herself—almost twelve years ago, and each piece was like an old loved friend. Even years later when Will, unsuccessful in finding the new start in life that he sought, rode off and never returned, leaving her near destitute, Lucilla refused to sell any of them.

She had survived, thanks to her skill with needle and thread, managing to raise Abby in a town where such was no easy accomplishment, and now she was looking forward to the day, soon to come, when the girl would marry Danny Stark, who worked for one of the big ranchers in the area.

Danny had a good job and fine prospects, and while Lucilla hated to see her daughter go, she would be vastly relieved when the marriage became a fact, for Abby would no longer be subjected to the dangers so prevalent in Lynchburg, since she would be living on the Laymon Ranch in the house provided for Danny.

Coming back around Lucilla crossed again to the window, once more peered eagerly out into the street. There was still no sign of Abby. Soft, even features darkening with concern, she moved back to the velvet-covered settee, sat down, and took up the hoop of embroidery she was working on.

In her mid-thirties Lucilla Roth still had a youthful appearance. Her skin was smooth and fair, and her light-blue eyes were bright with the look of vitality. There was no gray in her dark hair, gathered now in a bun on her neck, and her full figure drew far too much attention for her own comfort when she walked down the street.

Would she remain in Lynchburg after Abby was married and settled? Lucilla had considered the question often and at length in the past days, and was still undecided. The town had been a good place to live

when she and Will and their daughter had first arrived, but it had gone down terribly.

She'd really have no reason to stay other than to be
near Abby, and she guessed that was probably not as
important to her daughter, who would be busy with a
home life of her own, as she liked to think. It would
be nice to at last be free, move to another town, one
larger than Lynchburg, and maybe open another dressmaking shop, although, when she got down to the
bald truth, she was a bit weary of the struggle that
came with trying to make ends meet. It was too bad
that Major Bart Wagner, despite his arrogance and
often strange ways, wasn't single, and had ideas of
marriage. Being his wife, or of any officer at Fort
Shafter, meant a life of ease—and she certainly would
welcome that change with open arms.

But she'd never welcome Bart Wagner and the
proposal he'd made under any circumstance. A per-
sistent man, he had approached her several times on
the matter, evidently under the impression that he
could wear her down to where she would consent. In
fact, he was due to drop by that very evening, and
she could expect to hear from him the usual persua-
sive arguments.

A quick, businesslike rap on the door brought a
sigh to Lucilla's lips. It was Wagner's knock. Laying
aside the embroidery, she rose, crossed to the door,
and opened it, taking the opportunity to again glance
toward the street for some sign of Abby. A thought
came to her; she'd ask the officer to walk with her to
the Willcox house.

"I said good evening, Lucilla—" Wagner's slightly
indignant voice cut into her thoughts, bringing her
back to the moment.

She stepped away, allowed him to enter.

"Good evening, Bart. I was just looking to see if Abby was coming. I sent her on an errand, and she hasn't—"

"She'll be all right," Wagner broke in impatiently, ignoring the woman's fears. "And, frankly, I'm glad we're to be alone. We have to talk, settle things."

Lucilla closed the door quietly, turned, and placed her shoulders to it. "I don't know that there is anything to be settled."

Wagner, a tall, lean man, also in his mid-thirties, was in a clean, freshly pressed uniform and gleaming boots. He had just shaved, which left the skin of his narrow face with a rosy pinkness; his hair, dark and lustrous from pomade, had a precise side part, with the edges in perfect order. His eyes, somewhat small and also dark, were close set, and each time Lucilla looked at the man she was reminded of the ferret her brother had caught in a trap when they were children back in Michigan.

"You know exactly what I'm talking about!" he snapped. "We've been over it a dozen times—every time I've called on you, in fact."

"*You've* talked of it, Bart," Lucilla corrected softly. "And the answer is still no."

Wagner's shoulders stiffened. Reaching up, he released the top button of his coat and ran a finger around the inside of the collar. Beads of sweat were on his forehead just beneath the hairline, and more moisture glistened on his upper lip and along the line of his jaw.

"I refuse to take that as final," he said stubbornly. "You know what you mean to me, and frankly, I intend to have you! Don't you see how much better off you'll be? Can't I make you understand what all I could do for you?"

"I'm not—"

"You wouldn't have to continue with this—this dressmaking thing, working your fingers to the bone trying to please these old biddies who look down on you and—"

"Do you think they—and everyone else—wouldn't look down on me if I consented to be your woman, your camp-follower wife?"

"They might—but what difference would it make? And they wouldn't dare say anything. What's so wrong with such arrangements? The fact is, it's fairly common. Many officers whose wives choose to remain back East, or wherever the family home is, have a woman—a consort, I guess you might call her—living near their post."

"But not inside," Lucilla said. Such a point was neither here nor there with her, but she enjoyed putting the officer at a disadvantage.

"Well, no, you could hardly expect that. The wives of the other officers would, well, object—and the colonel, he's pretty straitlaced. But you'd have all the advantages—"

"Advantages?"

"Yes—food for one thing. I would keep you well-supplied with all the best that we, as officers, are privileged to have. I'd give you money, enough to satisfy your needs, within reason, of course. You'd never need to work again, that's for certain—unless you wished. And if you didn't want to continue living here, I could find you a place closer to Shafter—"

"One of those shacks outside, where the enlisted men keep their female companions—that what you mean?"

"Of course not! It wouldn't be fitting for an officer to be seen going there. What I had in mind, if you gave up this place, was a house—one near the fort. Or you could live in the hotel, the Posada, if you liked.''

Lucilla half-turned, listened, thinking she had heard footsteps in the street. She had, but it was someone walking rapidly toward the center of town.

Concern for Abby had now grown to major proportions. Something was wrong—there could be no doubt of that. Even Edith Willcox would not be so thoughtless as to detain the girl this long. She'd break off this tiresome conversation with Bart Wagner—doing so in a way that would not anger him too much—then appeal for his help in looking for Abby.

''And all I'd have to do for that is be available for bed any time you dropped by?''

Wagner's jaw tightened angrily at the sarcasm in the woman's tone, but he apparently figured he had everything to lose and nothing to gain by allowing it to surface.

''That's a bit crude,'' he said blandly. ''I wouldn't put it exactly in those terms.''

''Well, no matter how it's put, the meaning is still the same. But if you—''

Lucilla turned as hurried footsteps sounded on the hard-pack walk outside. Abby! Moving quickly, she threw open the door.

''Abby!'' she cried in alarm as the girl, disheveled, dress torn, eyes red from weeping, face streaked by tears, burst into the room. ''What happened?''

''Oh, Mother—it was terrible!''

Lucilla gathered her daughter into her arms, held her close. She feared the worst, long since aware that saddle tramps, soldiers, saloon bums, and like riffraff were abroad in the town after dark, but she'd not let herself believe what might have happened until Abby herself confirmed it.

"That horrible man—Jed they called him," the girl said between sobs. "He—he caught me, dragged me into the saloon, the one they call the Bull's Head—"

Lucilla's blood chilled. She glanced at Bart Wagner standing off to one side, a deep frown on his face, one of impatience at the interruption rather than concern for Abby, she suspected.

"Then a man standing at the bar stepped in and hit him and made him let me go. Then there was a fight—"

"Who was it that helped you?"

"I-I don't know. Just a man—a stranger."

Lucilla did her best to calm the girl, patting her gently, kissing her on the forehead and cheeks, all the while murmuring softly. Abby had not been harmed, and that was all that mattered—thanks to some stranger. If she could learn who he was—and he had to be a stranger if he was foolish enough to go up against Jed Bleeker—she'd thank him.

"Everything's all right now," she assured the girl. "Why don't you go to your room and lie down for a bit? We'll have supper later."

Abby, no longer racked by sobs, turned away at once and disappeared into the short hallway that led to her quarters next to the kitchen.

"That's one thing more," Bart Wagner said when he and Lucilla were again alone, "I'd see to it that the girl would not be molested. I'd order my men to keep an eye on her."

"There won't be any need for that, thank you. Abby plans to marry in a couple of weeks. I think now I'll set an earlier date so she can move away from here." Lucilla paused. "Not that I'm eager to get rid of her—it's just that I want her where she'll be safe."

The officer nodded slowly. "I understand . . . What's the boy's name? Do I know him?"

"It's doubtful, but he's Danny Stark. He works for Earl Laymon, the rancher."

"No, I don't recognize the name, but the fort does buy beef now and then from Laymon. And I do think you're smart in hurrying things along . . . I'd best be running along. With Powell still in Washington and Agnew out on maneuvers, I can't be away from Shafter for long."

Wagner's attitude seemingly had softened, and he had become more understanding. A smile parted his thin lips.

"I'll drop by again tomorrow evening," he said. "Think about my offer."

Lucilla's shoulders moved indifferently. "I can, but the answer will still be the same, Bart," she said, and opened the door for him to leave. "Good night."

"Good night," the officer responded stiffly, and hurrying past her, stepped out into the hushed night.

Wagner halted when he heard Lucilla Roth close the door and turn the lock. Standing behind a head-high lilac bush, he unbuttoned the rest of his coat, exposing his undershirt and allowing cool air to relieve the heat trapped against his body. He took a deep breath, enjoying the moment.

But he was far from being pleased where Lucilla was concerned—was, in fact, tired of her continual refusals. There was one thing, however, he prided himself on: he never gave up when he was after something he really wanted.

And Lucilla Roth was one woman he intended to have. All the others he'd known, including the mousy little woman who was his wife and whom he kept safely stowed away in far distant Richmond, could in no way ever match Lucilla in downright beauty of figure and face as well as in intelligence. He fairly ached when he envisioned her, unclothed, awaiting him in some cool, shadowy room hidden away from interruptions from the fort and everyone else.

And he now had the means by which he could satisfy that relentless desire, make it all come true. Danny Stark, Lucilla had said the name of the boy was whom she was eager to have her daughter marry. He worked for the rancher who supplied Shafter with beef on occasion. All well and good. He'd have a little talk with First Sergeant Gavin O'Hanlon when he got back to the fort, and put into effect the idea—a scheme—that had entered his mind when Lucilla was telling him of her wish to get her daughter married and out of Lynchburg as soon as possible.

If everything went as planned—and certainly there was no reason why it should not—Lucilla Roth would be all his before the week ended.

☆ **9** ☆

It had been shortly after midnight when Magatagan took leave of Dolly Jo Morrison's company. He had gone downstairs, had himself a final drink—the bottle he'd earlier bought long since empty—and making inquiries of Pete, the barkeep, as to the location of the town's only hotel, the Posada, made his way to it.

The place was not too bad, he found, was in fact a notch or two better than most frontier hostelries, and he had lost no time, after registering and being directed to a ground-floor room, in turning in. It was the first time in several weeks he would sleep in a spring bed, and with a roof rather than the starlit sky overhead.

Despite the lateness of his retiring, Reno was up before six o'clock, undergoing a cold shave and a wipe-down with water from the china bowl, after which he dressed. A man constantly on the trail, his wardrobe was necessarily limited, but he did have a clean shirt and socks available, and made use of both.

He'd as well ride on, he had decided earlier. There was nothing in Lynchburg to hold him, and while there'd been no sign of the rifleman on the sorrel horse, he could think of no good reason to delay crossing the border.

The same held true where friends of the Converse brothers were concerned. If there were any eager to take up the quarrel with him, they had not made themselves known that previous night in the Bull's Head, which could indicate there were none present in Lynchburg. Which left the possibility of their putting in an appearance that morning.

Magatagan considered the likelihood of that very slim; news simply did not travel that fast. He'd prefer to avoid them, anyway—not from any lack of confidence in himself should another shoot-out occur, but simply because he was still hopeful of keeping his gun in its holster. He'd find a restaurant, have himself a good breakfast, and move on.

Magatagan's thoughts along those lines came to a stop at that point when a knock sounded on the door. Strapping on his gun belt, he crossed the room to answer the summons; there was no need to wonder how anyone—friends of the Converse boys or the rider of the sorrel included—would know where he had put up for the night, as it was Pete, the Bull's Head bartender, who had directed him to the Posada.

One hand resting on the butt of his .44, Reno unlocked the thin panel. Then, opening it, he stepped back. A frown crossed his face. It was a woman and three men. One of the latter, a slightly built individual wearing a storekeeper's bib apron, nodded and extended his hand.

"Name's John Broome, Mr. Magatagan," he said as Reno responded to the greeting. "Own the general store. We'd like to have a word with you. It all right if we step in out of the hall?"

Reno moved aside to let his visitors in, and closed the door. A thin smile parted his lips as he sensed what their presence meant; the low regard in which townspeople held men of his calling was all too familiar. Coming about, he crossed his arms and considered them coolly.

"Something on your mind?"

The woman spoke up at once. "I'm Lucilla Roth. It was my daughter you helped last night. I came to thank you for that."

Magatagan's smile lost some of its iciness. "Was nothing much to it."

"Around here it was," Broome said, and then bobbed his head at the two men standing beside him. "Like for you to meet Ed Stone and Cal Beatty. Ed runs the feed-and-seed store. Cal's got a saloon down the street, calls it Beatty's Place."

Magatagan shook hands with both. Stone was probably in his fifties, as was Broome. He was dark, with a thick mustache and a square-cut beard. Beatty was also a man in that age bracket, had sandy-brown hair and light eyes. He was dressed in a gray suit complete with collar and tie.

But Reno gave the men only cursory attention, having difficulty in keeping his eyes off the woman, Lucilla Roth. Her daughter did look something like her, he saw, but the girl lacked the real beauty in both face and figure that her mother possessed, but he supposed such would come along later as the girl grew older. One thing certain, Mr. Roth was a most fortunate man to have a woman such as Lucilla for a wife.

"We'd like to talk with you—we've got sort of a proposition," Broome, apparently the spokesman, said.

"Aiming to ride out this morning," Magatagan replied, puzzled. "Doubt if I'd be interested in whatever you're thinking about."

Broome's expression changed, reflecting his disappointment. Cal Beatty frowned, brushed at his beard.

"Mighty sorry to hear that, but listen to us anyway. Maybe you'll change your mind."

"Doubt that, too, but go ahead."

Broome took heart from the response. His features
brightened. "First off, we best explain that what
happened to Lucilla's—Mrs. Roth's—girl last night
ain't nothing new around here. Been several cases
over the last year or two where girls have just up and
disappeared, and then were found later to be there on
the second floor of Monty Rand's place ruined and
too ashamed to go home."

"Truth is, no woman's safe out of her house at
night, be she young or old," Stone added. "Not
much better for a man either. Holdups and beatings
are plenty common." The feed merchant paused.
"You see, we ain't got no law here."

"What I hear. Seems nobody's running the town,
but everybody's wanting to," Magatagan said, eyes
on Lucilla. Erect, square-shouldered in a figured ging-
ham dress, she looked cool and provocative, and
seemed almost to be challenging him with her pale-
blue eyes.

"That's about the size of it," Broome agreed, and
then continued, "Lord help us if Rand and his bunch
ever get the upper hand!"

Magatagan was silent for a moment, listening to
the quick beat of riders passing in the street. Then,
"Why not make a deal with the army—get the provost marshal to take charge. I understand the town's
on the military reservation, anyway."

"We don't know that for sure," Edward Stone
said quickly. "Colonel Powell, the post commander, is back in Washington now trying to iron things

out. My guess is we'll be declared outside the reservation.''

"And turning things over to the army wouldn't be of much help," Broome said. "Actually, we'd be no better off. The fort's made up of malcontents and misfits of the worst kind, been shipped in here from a dozen other posts. They're no better than that bunch of outlaws Rand's got hanging around his place. If either bunch ever took over, it would be mighty bad for the townspeople—what few of us there are left.''

Magatagan shrugged, saying nothing but clearly conveying his wonder as to how any of it concerned him.

"We don't know where you're going—you haven't said—but we'd like to talk you into staying right here in Lynchburg," Lucilla Roth added when Broome had finished.

Her voice, Reno thought, exactly matched her appearance and personality. He felt a twinge of envy. Did her husband realize what a treasure he had? Personally, knocking about the country for years, he had encountered many attractive women, but he could recall none who came anywhere near Lucilla Roth where looks were concerned—and all else, too, probably. Being persuaded to hang around Lynchburg for her sake alone would be easy, if she wasn't married, and he didn't have good reason to keep moving.

"Right kind of you to say that, but I can't see—''

"What we're getting at," Broome cut in, "is we're offering you the job of town marshal.''

"I was in the Bull's Head last night and seen you handle them two hard cases that jumped you," Stone said.

"And we heard how you roughed up Jed Bleeker and made him leave Lucilla's girl be," Beatty added.

"We figure you're just the man we need, and want," Broome finished. "We'll pay whatever wages you want, within reason. What do you say?"

Reno Magatagan was at a loss for words. He—a lawman? With maybe a dozen or so marshals and sheriffs all anxious to lay their hands on him and drag him up before a judge somewhere; with perhaps half that many gunhands, such as the Converse brothers—not to overlook the rider on the sorrel—all just aching to put a bullet in him—he should pin on a star?

Magatagan shook his head and laughed.

☆ 10 ☆

An injured look crossed John Broome's features.
Stone and Beatty exchanged glances of frustration.
Lucilla Roth turned, stared out of the window, hiding
her feelings.

"Didn't intend for this to be no joke," Broome
said. "It's a mighty serious matter with us."

Reno's face sobered. "Joke's on me, not on you
folks," he said, reaching for his tobacco and papers,
shaping up a cigarette. "Right sorry if you took it
wrong, but me wearing a star struck me as funny."

Lucilla came back around. "Why would it?"

"Expect I know," Broome said before Magatagan
could make his own reply. "The law's after him."

Reno nodded, lit his smoke, exhaled a small blue
cloud, and studied the tip of his cigarette thoughtfully. He could see no reason for not being honest with
the woman and the men with her. He would be
across the line in Mexico before the morning was
over and beyond the reach of any lawman who might
get word of his being in Lynchburg.

"That's it," he said, attention on Lucilla Roth.
For some unaccountable reason he wanted to see her
reaction to what he intended to say. "I'm wanted in a
dozen states and territories for murder, robbery, and
holdup. Most of the charges ain't true, but there's no

convincing the law of that. I've never held up a stagecoach or robbed a man in my life, but because I was seen somewhere around, I got credit for it.''

"What about murder?'' the woman asked quietly.

"Not the way of it, either. I'll admit to shooting, killing, well, several men, but every time it was a fair fight—the same as it was with that pair, the Converse brothers, in the saloon last night.''

"Sure can't fault you there,'' Stone said. "They crowded you into it.''

"A few days back, in a town a ways north of here, I shot it out with one of their leading citizens. Killed him. That was a fair fight, too, but there are plenty who won't see it that way. They'll take the stand that he was just an ordinary man while I'm a gunfighter and he didn't have a chance. It won't matter, either, that he had it coming to him.''

Lucilla's features were taut, almost strained, and there was a brightness in her eyes—a look of horror, Reno thought. But he wanted her to know what he was—not that it mattered all that much, since he would shortly be riding on—but yet, within him, something was craving understanding on her part.

"If it was justified, I don't see how—''

"Once a man gets a reputation with a gun, there's no changing back. It's like the mark of Cain—you never get rid of it.''

Silence followed Magatagan's words. The men looked down, shifted nervously on their feet. Lucilla Roth made some unnecessary adjustments with the trim of her collar, while outside in the street the somewhat thick voice of a man, evidently well in his cups, could be heard shouting something to another.

"Why did you kill this man, the one in the town north of here?'' Lucilla broke the hush finally. "You said he deserved it. Seems to me the law ought to bear that in mind.''

"Was a family matter—and the law doesn't hold with that. I'd hunted him for years, and when I found him, I did what I had to. Was hoping that would be the last time I'd use my gun, but the hope didn't last long."

"Can't blame yourself for shooting them two last night," Stone said, repeating himself. "They forced it."

Magatagan scarcely noticed the feed-store man's effort to comfort him, his attention still being on Lucilla Roth. There had been a slight break in the stiffness of her manner, a softening, he thought, as if she had found a bit of sympathy and understanding for him.

It was Broome, however, who spoke. "Well, dammit, I don't see that any of what you said matters to us!" he declared in a voice unnecessarily loud. "We need a good man who's able to not only take care of himself, but keep the outlaws and rowdies that are hanging around here in line. And far as I'm concerned, you're him."

"Amen to that," Cal Beatty murmured feelingly.

"Putting it frank and flat out, we need a hard case like you," Stone said, and added hastily, "Meaning no offense, of course! What I'm trying to make you understand is that it'll take a man that's not only had a lot of experience dealing with outlaws and riffraff and the like, but one who can stay alive doing it."

"This was once a plenty nice little town," Broome said after there was no comment from Magatagan. "Folks could raise their children without being afraid something bad would happen to them, same as they felt easy about coming and going anywhere around here, day or night.

"Nowadays, since the army's moved in and Monty Rand's opened up his place and took on a bunch of outlaws to look after his interests, it ain't hardly safe to even leave your house."

"You seen that with Lucilla's girl," Stone reminded.

"And Lucilla can tell you a few things herself about how it is to be a single woman in this town," Broome said.

A single woman . . . Magatagan frowned, looked more closely at Lucilla Roth. A slight pink lifted in her cheeks when she realized what his thoughts were.

"Oh, I had a husband, but he's gone now," she said. "And what Ed and John have said is the truth. No woman is safe around here after dark—especially if she doesn't have a man. I'm not taking any more chances with Abby. We had planned on her getting married later on, but after what happened last night we've moved up the date."

"Sure don't blame you, Lucilla," Broome said. "The girl'll be better off out there on Laymon's ranch than in town—the way things are going."

"Ain't sure what you're holding off for," Ed Stone said, facing Magatagan and coming back to the point, "but if you're scared of some lawman dropping by and spotting you, you can plain forget it. Ain't no man wearing a star been by here since the army moved in. Guess they figure it's up to the soldiers to look after Lynchburg."

"Probably," Reno said. "Usually the way of it."

"If Colonel Powell ever gets things squared around back there in Washington, I expect that's how it'll be, but he sort of warned us before he left that it'll take a long time to iron out the mess and that we'll just have to make the best of it until then.''

"Now, if any jackleg lawman or bounty hunter does come along looking for you," Broome said, again after a pause in the conversation, "it'd be you deciding what to do about them—jug them, run them out of town, or whatever. You'll be the only law in this town, and what you do will be jake with us— same as it will be with the rest of the decent folks living here.''

Once more a hush filled the small room, growing stuffy now from the rising heat. Somewhere off to the west of town two gunshots sounded in rapid succession.

"We'd sure like to hear your answer now," Broome said. There was a note of desperation in his voice.

"And if you ain't interested," Beatty added, "we just ain't sure what we'll do. Things are getting worse every day.''

"That's the gospel truth!" Stone declared. "There'll be a lot of fine people beholden to you if you can see your way clear to help us. What do you say? Will you take the job?''

☆ **11** ☆

Magatagan smiled again, the irony of the situation once more striking him as amusing. What a joke it would be on the lawmen searching for him! But he could see there was nothing humorous insofar as the good people of Lynchburg were concerned.

He supposed he could accept the job—on a temporary basis, of course. A few more days would make little if any difference. Too, he was near the border, could cross over in a matter of hours if necessary. Besides—Magatagan's shuttered eyes were fixed on Lucilla Roth—he'd like to get to know her better.

He wasn't exactly sure in his own mind which was taking precedence: the town's crying need for help or his interest in the woman who was studying him so coolly from brow-shadowed blue eyes. He guessed it didn't matter. A man lived but one time, and it was only smart to make the best of what came his way.

"Can't see anything wrong with taking the job—for a while, anyway," he said. "We can—"

Reno got no further. John Broome, a wide smile wreathing his face, rushed forward, hand outstretched.

"That's good—real good—fine!" the merchant said fervently. "Everybody in town 'cepting Rand's bunch and a lot of them soldiers are going to be mighty happy about this!"

Stone stepped up beside Broome, seized Magatagan's hand also. "You won't ever be sorry you're doing this for us! And we'll make it right with you. We'll get together first off, figure what kind of wages to pay, and—"

"No hurry," Magatagan said, glance on Lucilla, now smiling her thanks and approval, as he took the congratulations of Cal Beatty. "Whatever you pay your regular lawman will be all right with me."

"Forty a month and keep?" Broome said in a shocked voice. "No, sir—we'll do better than that!"

"Suit yourself," Reno answered. "It all right if I forget about wearing a star?"

Broome shook his head. "I don't understand—"

"It'd make me feel sort of funny. I've always been on the wrong side of the fence when it comes to lawmen—"

"I don't see that it'd matter, John," Ed Stone said quickly, as if fearing Magatagan might change his mind. "Won't take more'n a couple of hours for everybody around to hear about him being the new marshal, so a badge won't count for nothing anyway."

"Guess you're right," Broome said, and nodded to Magatagan. "I'll have to give you the oath, though. We want everything you do—and have to do—to be legal. That agreeable?"

Magatagan signified that it was, tossed aside the butt of his cigarette, now dead, took out his makings, and started to roll another.

"Place for you to do your living in the back of the marshal's office," Broome continued. "Ain't much, but you'll find it comfortable. Jail's on the back of the lot, real handy. Now you take your meals at Phil Perkins' Restaurant, just down the street a piece.

Keep your horse at Lige Crow's Livery Stable. Town'll be paying for both.''

"Sounds like a right handy setup," Magatagan said, lighting his fresh smoke. "Want to be sure we all understand one thing, however. I'll clean up your town my way. I'm no lawman, so I probably won't be doing it the way they would, but I'll get the job done."

"You'll have a free hand," Broome assured.

"Could be some folks'll think I'm a bit too hard and will want me to back off a bit," Reno continued. "Best they get it straight in their head that a man can't do that, otherwise he loses what he's gained."

"Leaving everything up to you," Broome said, looking at Stone and Beatty. "You do what you figure you have to. The rest of the town'll approve— don't you fret none about that."

"I don't aim to favor somebody's friend, either—"

"Won't be none of that," Stone declared. "Like John said, you've got a free hand to do what you have to."

"Expect that gets everything squared away, then," Magatagan said. "Might remind you that since I don't figure to be around long, you best find a deputy to work with me—not so much that I'll be needing one, but I could sort of break him in on the job and get folks used to having him around."

"That'd be a good idea, for sure," Broome agreed. "I don't know who we could get—nobody around here has ever wanted the job—but maybe all that'll change, so we'll be trying. Meantime, if you run across a man you figure'd make a good marshal, just go ahead and hire him."

Broome turned away, started toward the door. He paused, allowed Lucilla to move in ahead of him while Beatty and Stone fell in behind. Reaching the panel, he halted, looked back.

"Soon as it's to your liking drop by my store. I'll swear you in—officially."

A slight grin parted Magatagan's lips as the paradox once again occurred to him. Being sworn in to uphold the law, considering the life he'd led, didn't make much sense! But he had agreed—perhaps in a moment of weakness, now that he thought of it—to take on the job, and he'd stand by his word.

"Can look for me in an hour or so," he said. "Need to get a bite to eat—and maybe do a bit more fixing up."

"Told you about Phil Perkins'—get your breakfast there," Broome said. "Barber shop's right next door, if you're wanting a bath and such."

"Expect I better look my best," Reno said, and watched Broome open the door, after which they all filed out into the semidark hallway.

The scarred panel had scarcely closed when a knock sounded again. Magatagan crossed the room and, grasping the knob, drew it open. Pleasure spread across his hard features. It was Lucilla Roth.

"Come in," he invited, stepping back.

The woman complied at once, but halted just within the doorway. Her skin was smooth, had a soft, ivory look, he noticed as she faced him, and her lips were full and near perfectly shaped.

"I just happened to think, Mr. Magatagan—"

"Reno," he broke in. "Never am real sure if it's me somebody's talking to when they call me mister."

She smiled, her eyes twinkling. "All right, Reno, and I'm Lucilla—or Lucy, if you like."

"Lucilla—that sounds right pretty to me—"

The smile widened. Then, "What I came back for

was to ask you if you'd care to come by this evening and have supper with us—Abby and me. I expect you're plenty tired of restaurants and your own cooking.''

''For a fact,'' Magatagan said. ''I'll be real pleased to eat with you and your daughter.''

''Then it's settled,'' Lucilla said, her face reflecting her pleasure. ''We eat about six o'clock. Will that be all right with you?''

''Be just fine—''

''Good. I'll see you at that time,'' Lucilla said, and again passed through the doorway into the hall and beyond Magatagan's view.

He remained motionless for a long minute, remembering the look of her, enjoying the faint odor of perfume that still remained, and then rousing himself, he pushed the door shut. A vague sense of reproval was building within him; Lucilla Roth was a good woman, a fine one, in fact, and he was showing too much interest in her and she in him.

Hell, within maybe a week or so he'd be moving on, actually running for his life if he cared to face the truth, and where would that leave her? She had already lost one man, her husband, somehow, and to sort of push things along between himself and the woman was all wrong. He frowned. Maybe it wasn't! Lucilla had been told who and what he was and where he was headed—that he'd soon be on his way. Aware of all that and being a grown woman, she knew what she was doing, he reckoned.

But he couldn't be sure, Reno decided, taking up his hat and turning to leave. She was a fine woman and didn't deserve to be hurt. From then on, he'd be mighty careful of what he said and how he acted around her.

Leaving the hotel, Magatagan, conscious of the glances turned upon him by the scatter of persons along the street, went first to Perkins' Restaurant and had himself a meal of bacon, eggs, biscuits, and coffee—all of which was being taken care of by the town council, Perkins, a small, wisp of a man with deep-set eyes and a nervous, birdlike manner, assured him.

Hunger satisfied, Magatagan then entered the nearby barber shop, where he treated himself to a hot bath and a haircut, after which he returned to the street. Again aware of the attention paid him not only by persons along the sidewalks, but by those watching from windows, he bent his steps for John Broome's General Store.

"Get rid of that bastard," Monty Rand said in a hard, flat voice, leaning forward in his chair.

Jed Bleeker nodded. "Hell, you ain't wanting him dead no more'n I am!"

"I'm leaving it up to you and Mason. Bring in Idaho and Mora if it's too big a job for you."

"Ain't no need," Bleeker grumbled. "I can take care of him."

Rand settled back. "You sure couldn't last night," he observed dryly.

"The son of a bitch just caught me not looking. Be different next time I come across him."

The saloon owner folded his arms across his chest and winked slyly at Charlie Mason, the big man he kept behind the bar as a preventative against the Bull's Head patrons getting out of hand and breaking up the furniture. Rand had called the pair into his office only minutes earlier to let them know what he wanted done.

·"I want something done today," Rand continued. "Either find a way to put a bullet into him or run him out of town. I don't want him sticking his nose in my business again."

"Well, he ain't leaving town—no, sir! He ain't going nowhere 'cepting to the boneyard," Bleeker declared. "I owe him aplenty, and he's sure going to get paid in full!"

"Suit yourself—just get at it," Monty said, and then added, "But don't fool yourself, Jed, about him. He's no saddle bum that you can slap around anyway you please. He'll kill you if you look cross-eyed at him! You and Charlie had better get together with Mora and Idaho and figure out some way to take care of him."

Bleeker gave that thought and shrugged. "Don't figure I'll be needing any help, but Charlie here can come along if he's of a mind. Aim to start looking for him right soon, quick as I get a couple of chores done, and—"

Bleeker paused as the door to the office opened and Pete the bartender appeared. Hand still grasping the china knob, he nodded.

"Figured you'd want to know this, Monty," he said. "Word's out that Magatagan—he's the jasper that cold-cocked Jed and shot them two drifters here last night—has took on the job as town marshal."

Walking leisurely down the street en route to Broome's store, Reno Magatagan took note of Lynchburg. Like a hundred other towns he'd been in, it consisted of one main street along which ranged, shoulder to shoulder and facing one another from across the dusty roadway, some three dozen or so business buildings—about half of which appeared to him to be vacant.

It was too bad the stagecoach company had pulled out, he thought. Judging from the empty structures staring hollow-eyed at one another from opposite sides of the canyonlike street, their faded signs almost illegible from time and bullet holes, Lynchburg once had been a prosperous and most likely a steadily growing settlement. Now, its principal reason for life being gone, it was only a shell of its former self, kept alive by the few hardy souls who refused to admit defeat, the saloon and outlaw element, and the soldiers from the nearby post—there because they had no choice.

Magatagan came to a stop in front of Broome's. Large, sprawling, with a landing that extended the building's width and thrust toward the street for half that distance, the store evidently had once enjoyed a thriving patronage. A solitary horse stood at the hitch-

ing rack fronting the empty wagon yard. Taking note
of the animal—a fine, big black with a heavy, A-fork
double-rigged saddle and silver mounted bridle, both
almost new—Reno mounted the steps to the landing,
crossed to the screen door, and entered the building.

John Broome, in the rear with several men not
distinguishable in the shadowy interior, came forward at once, hand extended.

"Mighty glad you've come," he greeted. "Not
everybody here that I was hoping for, but I reckon it
won't matter. Come on back, and I'll make you
acquainted."

Reno followed the merchant to the rear of the
store, idly noticing the thinly stocked shelves, and
halted before the group of men. Ed Stone he knew;
the feed-and-seed dealer offered his hand again, after
which Broome turned to the others.

"This here's Earl Laymon—owns the biggest ranch
in these parts," he said, pointing to a heavyset,
solid-looking individual with graying hair, but coal-
black mustache, dressed in cattleman's clothing. "He
speaks for all the ranchers around here."

"Pleased to meet you," Laymon said, grasping
Reno's hand in a firm clasp. "John's told me all
about you. I'm expecting you to clean up this town—
get rid of all the no-accounts and hard cases."

Magatagan, not too taken by the rancher's imperi-
ous manner, shrugged. "Figure to do what I can."

"This here's Lige Crow," Broome continued, bob-
bing at a lanky, bearded man with small sharp eyes,
clad in undershirt, bib overalls, and heavy shoes.
"Runs the livery stable."

Crow grinned, exposing large, tobacco-stained teeth,
and greeted Magatagan warmly. "Sure glad you've

took up with us, friend! Can count on me to side you all the way.''

At that moment Cal Beatty entered in company with Perkins, the restaurant owner. Broome eyed them briefly as if chiding them for being tardy and then, moving in behind the counter that extended almost entirely across the back of the room, produced a small metal box. Opening it, he took a star from among several folded documents and handed it to Magatagan.

''Know you ain't for wearing this, but you best carry it on you—in your pocket. Just might need it. Now, being the mayor of this town, and with most of the council present, I hereby appoint you the marshal. Good luck.''

Magatagan smiled wryly, dropped the star in his vest pocket. Luck wouldn't have a whole lot to do with his getting the job done, he realized. It would more to being quick and handy with the gun he carried, and in not backing away from the hard-case element that frequented the Bull's Head and the ungovernable soldiers from close by Fort Shafter. One thing, his hope of hanging up his .44 was gone—at least for the time being. He hadn't thought of that earlier, but the swearing in by Broome and the star given him brought that home to him now.

''Goes for me, too,'' he heard Lige Crow add, after which Laymon, Stone, Beatty, and Perkins made known their well wishes.

He had half-expected Lucilla Roth to be present, and a twinge of disappointment trickled through him when he saw that the woman was absent. But, he supposed, not being a member of the town council, she was not requested to attend. He'd see her at supper that night, anyway, Reno reminded himself.

"John was telling me about this free hand you're claiming you have to have," Laymon said. "Now, I'm not so sure that's a smart idea. We sure don't want no war."

Reno, lips curling slightly, reached for the star in his vest pocket.

"Hold on!" Broome cried in alarm. "Don't go flying off the handle. Earl ain't meaning that you ought to go easy on that riffraff bunch. It's just that—"

"Laymon's not speaking for all of us," Ed Stone cut in angrily. "Far as we're concerned—and we're the majority of the council—you've got your free hand. You do whatever you figure you have to."

Magatagan pivoted slowly to the rancher. "Only way I'll take the job is to have all of you backing me."

Laymon was quiet for several moments while he brushed at the corners of his black mustache. "All right," he said gruffly. "But let's get this straight—it'll be your doing if things get out of hand and we end up worse off than we were at the start."

"That won't ever happen," John Broome stated quietly.

"But you sure'n hell can't guarantee that—"

The storekeeper laughed ruefully. "Hell, Earl, there ain't no guarantee on nothing anymore—not since the war. We're at the point where we've got to gamble on staying alive or dying off like a lot of other towns around here have. And our best bet to keep from doing that is a marshal with enough guts to clean out the place. Maybe folks'll start moving back when they hear what's going on."

"You're forgetting we maybe don't have a town if Powell comes back from Washington with orders to move everybody off the—"

"We'll cross that creek when we come to it," Broome interrupted crisply. "I'm not so sure it'll turn out that way. What all them high muckity-mucks back there in Washington best bear in mind is that the town was here first, and that old man Lynch's papers were all in good order."

"Won't deny that, but the fact is, according to Wagner, the major that's running the fort while Powell's away, it was a military reservation before Lynch settled on it. The fort just hadn't been built yet."

"Wagner's a snake-oil peddler, far as I'm concerned," Ed Stone said, and spat into a nearby sandbox provided for the purpose. "I wouldn't believe nothing he said was he to swear on a stack of Bibles nine feet high!"

"I've done a little business with him," Laymon said, frowning. "Always seemed pretty straight to me."

Stone laughed. "Straight? Hell, if he ever gives you an apple, you best look for a worm because it'll sure have one in it."

The rancher shrugged, shifted his attention to Reno. "Well, no matter how this all sounds, Marshal, I'm all for you. And you can figure on me standing by you no matter what."

Magatagan nodded. "Obliged to you," he said with no particular feeling, and then added, "Reckon I'd best get about my business."

"You'll be wanting to see your office and where you'll be roosting," Lige Crow said. "Be real pleased to show you—it's right near my place."

"I'll take it as a favor," Reno said, and touching the other men with his glance, he turned and followed the livery-stable owner to the door.

☆ **13** ☆

Major Bart Wagner stood at the window of post headquarters and stared gloomily down at Fort Shafter's parade ground. His office, or rather that of Colonel Newton Powell, occupied a small room placed atop the long, flat administration building, which forever reminded the officer of the apt but derogatory description of a Union warship used so effectively in the war—a cheesebox on a raft. But it was a good arrangement, nevertheless, as it permitted an overall view of the entire post along with the surrounding area.

Directly below, in the same building, were other offices, workshops, and storage and supply rooms. Fronting headquarters lay the parade, while on its opposite side stood the hospital. The enlisted men's barracks were to the left, the officer's quarters to the right, and a short distance from the latter was the three-room cottage where Colonel Powell lived.

On beyond were the mess hall and kitchen, the guardhouse, sutler's store, and various other buildings. The stables were back of administration, the odors from which were only too familiar to persons inside, thanks to a prevailing west wind.

It was a plan he certainly would not have approved had he been consulted on the construction of Shafter,

Wagner had thought often; but then he didn't know the right people or have the connections back in Washington to ever be in on anything of importance. He was just an officer who had been plucked from a comfortable post in West Virginia and sent to this God-forsaken hell-hole at the end of civilization where there was nothing but heat, sand, wind, ignorance, and disease.

Bart Wagner considered it an insult and a terrible injustice to a man of his quality, but as a career officer he had accepted it—immediately upon arrival doing what he could to effect a transfer. But he struggled to make the best of a disagreeable situation, the success of which depended almost completely on a woman named Lucilla Roth.

If he could persuade her to become his pigeonhole wife, as the current and popular term among officers went, he'd be able to stomach, at least for a time, the unpleasant life thrust upon him. The woman had resisted so far, but he guessed he'd found the means to persuade her to see things his way, at last. It was mean and underhanded, but in such situations all was fair, and after all, no one would get hurt—just scared.

Wagner brushed at the sweat on his forehead. Where the devil was O'Hanlon? Thinking of Lucilla had quickened his pulse and heightened his impatience to have the woman. He'd sent for the sergeant a good quarter-hour ago after dispatching the adjutant to the post surgeon's office, where he would keep busy for a time searching through records—a purely unnecessary task that would get the man from underfoot—while he outlined to the sergeant what he wanted done.

Dammit! If O'Hanlon didn't show up in another thirty seconds, he'd—Wagner's anger lowered as he

saw the beefy figure of the noncom emerge from the
barracks and angle toward the administration building. About time, Wagner thought, and he'd not forget that O'Hanlon had kept him waiting. He'd let it
pass this time, however, but only because he needed
the man. Moving back to the chair behind the table
that served as a desk for Powell, Bart Wagner sat
down.

Almost at the same moment First Sergeant Gavin
O'Hanlon entered the room. A large, dark-haired
man with sharp eyes and a trailing, tobacco-stained
mustache, he stepped up before Wagner and saluted
smartly.

"Yes, sir—"

"You can dispense with the salute, Sergeant,"
Wagner said, wanting to put the situation on a more
equal, soldier-to-soldier basis. "I've got a small personal problem I need your help in handling."

O'Hanlon's broad face didn't change expression.
An old hand at the game, he was never surprised by
the things officers did.

"Yes, sir. Only glad to help, sir."

"No need to be so formal, O'Hanlon," Wagner
said, slightly irritated by the noncom's continued
observance of military courtesy. "That woman friend
of yours—will she do anything you ask?"

"Expect so," O'Hanlon said, now frowning. "What
is it you'll be needing from her?"

"I think she has a daughter of fifteen, or maybe
sixteen years old."

"A daughter she has, but she's just a younker.
About seven, as I recollect."

Wagner shrugged. "No problem. Now, here's what
I'm up against—and if a word of this gets out,
Sergeant, I'll have your stripes! Understand?"

"Yes, sir—"

"There's a lady in town that I'm very much interested in, but she's reluctant to see things my way. I've come up with a means for forci—getting her to make up her mind. Do you follow me, Sergeant?"

"Yes, sir. You're wanting her to be your pigeonhole wife, and she needs a shove."

Bart Wagner nodded slowly. "That's getting to the point, but it will take a little fancy maneuvering. She has a daughter that she wants very much to marry one of the local civilians—a boy named Danny Stark. Do you happen to know him?"

"Yes, sir, matter of fact, I do. He works for that rancher Laymon that we buy beef from. He's been one of the cowhands that drove in stock for us once or—"

"Good—that solves that part of my problem. Now the lady—you might as well know her name—is Mrs. Lucilla Roth."

O'Hanlon's thick brows lifted. "The dressmaker? She's a real looker, sir, if you don't mind me saying so."

"You're right, and I don't mind. Now, she's real anxious for the girl, her name's Abby, to marry this Danny Stark. Abby almost got in trouble yesterday walking by the Bull's Head, and Mrs. Roth figures if she can get her married off and out of town, her worries about something bad happening to the girl will be over."

"I can see that, but just how—where—"

"My plan is to create a problem for Mrs. Roth, one that only I can straighten out."

O'Hanlon smiled faintly. "And the price for you doing that is for her to see things your way—"

"Exactly," Wagner said, settling back into his

chair. "That's putting it a bit crudely, but you get the idea. Sometimes it's necessary to give someone a bit of a push to get them started in the right direction—you know that, Sergeant."

"Yes, sir, for certain I do, Major. Still don't see where me or my woman fits in—"

"Just this. I want her to accuse this Danny Stark of assault—rape—after which she'll file a complaint with you, and you will then arrest the boy, bring him here, and put him in the guardhouse. Since we're on a military reservation, Stark, if found guilty before a military court, could be sentenced to a firing squad. It won't go that far, of course."

O'Hanlon looked away and then nodded understandingly. "You'll be having a little talk with Mrs. Roth, telling her you'll step in and get the boy off—if she'll see things your way, I take it."

Wagner smiled. "You might say I'll be using a bit of friendly persuasion. You think you can arrange it with your lady friend to go along with the plan?"

O'Hanlon shrugged. "She will—or I'll whale the hell out of her. When does the major want me to start all this?"

"Today," the officer said immediately. "Get at it this morning, in fact. It has to be done before the girl and Stark are married."

"Easy to see why you're in a hurry, considering the lady concerned," O'Hanlon observed, "and I sure don't blame you." All pretense of military rank and courtesy was now missing from the noncommissioned officer's attitude. "With something like the dressmaker to—"

"Never mind, Sergeant. Just get busy—"

"Yes, sir," O'Hanlon replied, remembering his place. "Do I have your permission to leave the post?"

"You do, and I'll expect to hear—favorably—from you before retreat."

"You will that," O'Hanlon promised, and pivoting, moved across the room to the door. Opening it, he turned into the stairway and disappeared.

Bart Wagner, a satisfied glow filling him, rose, and with the solid thump of Gavin O'Hanlon's boot heels reaching his ears as the noncom descended the steps, walked again to the window that overlooked the parade grounds. The sergeant appeared, turned immediately, and headed for the stables. Wagner smiled tightly. Just be patient a little longer, old son, he consoled himself. The lady will soon be all yours.

☆ **14** ☆

The office provided for a town marshal wasn't too bad, Magatagan saw when he and Lige Crow reached the squat, flat-roofed building, a short distance west of the livery stable.

The main front-room area was fairly large and contained the usual rolltop desk, chair, benches along its walls, and the customary gun rack, empty at the moment. An out-of-date calendar supplied by a brewery in Kentucky was the only decoration, and everything was covered with a thick gray coating of dust.

"I'll send one of my boys over here and sweep out the place," Crow said, stepping to the door and releasing a stream of tobacco juice into the sun-baked soil beyond the landing in front of the building. "Now, back here's where you'll do your living."

Magatagan followed the stable owner through a doorway in the rear wall of the office into a darkened area. Crow released the shades on the two windows and admitted a flood of morning sunlight.

"Ain't much," Crow said apologetically, "but it'll look a sight better once it's cleaned up."

Magatagan nodded. A bed, chair, table, a two-lid stove that served for both heating and cooking and a wardrobe for clothing. Simple, basic, but all he would need for the short time he intended to be around.

"It'll do fine," Reno said. "Let's have a look at the jail."

"Right out the back," Crow replied, and led the way to another low, flat-roofed structure constructed of adobe.

It was a sturdy, serviceable building with two cells furnished only with slat cots; it had bars on its lone window and a thick, iron-reinforced door.

"Ain't nobody ever busted out of there," Lige said as they returned to the outside. There was a note of pride in his voice. And then he added somewhat sheepishly, "Of course there ain't hardly been nobody in it since it was built."

"There a key to that door?" Magatagan asked, attention drawn to several men standing at the rear of the Bull's Head watching him and Crow closely. Some of Rand's hard cases, no doubt.

"Sure. You'll find it in your desk, along with the ones to the cells. . . . You leave your animal at the barn behind the saloon?"

"Yes," Magatagan said, eyes still on the men. "Stabled him there when I rode in."

"I'll fetch him, take him to my barn," Lige said. "Expect you'd best do your own moving from the Posada."

"What I'll do," Reno said, "but first off, I've got a little business to take care of in Rand's place."

Crow scratched at his jaw, glanced toward the saloon. The men grouped around the building's rear entrance continued to stare. "Them's some of the gunnies Monty keeps hanging around to do his dirty work. What've you got in mind?"

"Let them, and everybody else around there, know that the town's got itself a marshal," Magatagan said, starting for the saloon. "Years ago it didn't take

me long to learn that the man who made the first
move at a time like this was the one who usually
comes out on top.''

"I reckon you're sure right," Crow said, again
shooting a line of brown juice into the dust. "You
want some company?"

"Obliged to you, but no." The men had turned,
were now entering the saloon by its rear door, Reno
noted. "It's my job—I'll handle it," he added, and
moved on.

Reaching the steps that led up to the Bull's Head's
back entrance, Magatagan paused, weighed the ad-
visability of entering. The men he had seen could be
expecting him and just might be waiting inside for
him to appear—if they were out to put a bullet in
him, which they could have in mind to do if they'd
already heard of his taking on the marshal's job.

Magatagan shrugged. He'd best not fool himself;
they would know—and they had seen him inspecting
the jail and the marshal's office. Likely, at that very
moment they were reporting such to Monty Rand.

A hard grin, one half-amused, half-regretful, pulled
at Reno's mouth. He wondered if he'd been stupid to
take on the job as lawman of a town torn in a
three-way fight for control, as was Lynchburg.

Being a marshal or a sheriff was always the farthest
thing from his mind; his intentions, since the day
he'd strapped on a gun and set out to find Henry
Bigbee, had run contrary to the law, as had his
thinking. But he had agreed to take on the task—
mostly because of Lucilla Roth, he had to admit—so
he'd go through with it. Perhaps, having been on the
side of the lawless would prove to be of some advantage to him; he'd always have a pretty good idea of
how an outlaw's mind would work.

"You for certain you ain't wanting me to side you, Marshal?"

It was Lige Crow's voice. Magatagan half-turned, glanced at the stable owner, who was headed for the saloon's barn a dozen or so yards on to the rear. As before, he declined the offer, grateful for it but knowing it could lead to serious trouble for Crow later on, should things not go right. Grasping the knob of the door before which he stood, Reno yanked the panel open and, hand resting on the butt of his .44, stepped quickly inside.

There was no one nearby in the foyerlike area into which he had entered. On ahead a short distance was the saloon proper. He could hear the rumble of talk indicating that the Bull's Head was enjoying a fair patronage even so early in the day. To his right was the short hallway at the end of which was a door. Rand's office, he recalled, remembering what he had learned the previous night. That was where he most likely would find the saloon owner as well as the hired guns Monty Rand kept hanging around.

Turning, he started for the door when motion in the direction of the saloon caught his eye. It was Dolly Jo. Dressed now in an ankle-length yellow dress, hair gathered on top of her head, she was frowning as she considered him. It was apparent she thought it unwise for him to be there. Reno smiled and continued toward Rand's quarters.

Reaching the door, he listened briefly to the sound of voices beyond the light panel, and then, taking a firm grip on the knob, he flung open the door and entered.

Rand was sitting at his desk. Jed Bleeker and the men he'd seen outside were standing before him. As Magatagan burst into the room, Bleeker made a stab for the weapon at his side. Magatagan's cold words chilled his intentions.

"Touch that gun and I'll kill you!"

Silence followed the warning. Bleeker slowly lifted his arms to show he had no further thought of drawing his pistol. Immediately the other men beside him followed his example. Rand, an angry frown on his sallow features, came fully about in his chair.

"What the hell do you want?"

"Giving you a little advice," Reno replied coolly. "I'm serving notice on you now that this town's got law, and I aim to enforce it."

"So I hear—"

"If you ever try shanghaiing another girl or woman for your bawdy house upstairs, or I hear of you rolling a drunk or one of your hired guns tricking a man into a shoot-out, I'll burn this damn place to the ground. That clear?"

Rand's expression did not change. And then, his attitude changing from one of belligerence to cooperation, he said, "Why, sure, Marshal. Long as you're around I'll do just what you say."

There was hidden meaning in the saloon man's words that did not escape Reno Magatagan. He reacted immediately.

"Something else. I want these two-bit gunhawks gone by morning. You won't need them anymore—so get rid of them."

Rand frowned, brushed angrily at some cigar ashes on the front of his shirt. He shook his head "You're overstepping yourself there. I don't have to—"

"Can tell you right now you do—unless you'd rather bury them." Magatagan stood motionless for a long minute as he allowed his words to have their full effect. Then, giving Bleeker and the men with him a warning glance, he turned about and, deliberately placing his back to them and Monty Rand, retraced his steps to the door. Halting there, hand on the knob, he looked over a shoulder.

"Tomorrow morning," he repeated, "and you'd best keep them out of my sight till then."

Opening the door, he stepped out into the hall.

☆ 15 ☆

Magatagan was taut, but a coolness was coursing through him. He'd made his first decisive move—as well make his presence and intentions clear to the patrons of the Bull's Head while he was there. Turning right at the end of the corridor, Reno walked quickly into the center of the saloon and halted.

A half-dozen patrons were at the bar, behind which was Pete. Near him was the big man, Charlie Mason, who was charged with quieting disturbances. Several men were at the faro game, and an equal number of soldiers were at a table trying their luck at poker with a sleazy-looking gambler. Two of the gaudily dressed girls hovered over them, but Reno saw no sign of Dolly Jo.''

Magatagan stood quietly while the steady flow of noise within the saloon dwindled and ceased as the Bull's Head's customers became aware of his presence. When all was silence except for sounds outside in the street and in the back rooms, Reno calmly drew his pistol and, pointing it at the floor, fired a bullet into the thick planking. Then, with the smell of burned powder spreading through the saloon and wisps of smoke curling about him, he nodded to the crowd.

''Remember that shot. Means this town's got a lawman now—me.''

Monty Rand, with Jed Bleeker, had appeared at the far end of the bar, coming quickly in response to the gunshot. Eyeing them coldly for a few moments, Magatagan again put his attention on the persons in the room.

"This town's got laws—most of you don't seem to know that. Can figure on them being enforced from now on, and if there's any of you that don't cotton to the idea, right now's the time to ride on. Goes for gunhands, cardsharps, panhandlers, and high-rollers. And any man I find bothering a woman will wind up in jail for a couple of years."

Silence followed Reno's words, and then a voice coming from somehwere in the casino part of the saloon spoke up.

"Hell, there ain't no such law that says a man has to do—"

"I say it—and I'm the law," Magatagan cut in sharply. "And if you want to argue about it, I'm willing to accommodate you anytime. Want this made clear, too. I won't stand for no fighting in the street or drunks laying around in public—"

"Just who give you leave to take over this here town?" a man in cattleman's clothes, wide-brimmed hat pushed to the back of his head as he sprawled in a chair, demanded. "Way I hear it the army's running this town."

"You heard wrong. The town was here first, and until I'm told different, I'll do what the folks who hired me want me to do."

"Your law don't apply to us soldiers," a heavyset, thick-shouldered man in a wrinkled, stained uniform declared. The single chevron of a private on the sleeve of his soiled shirt, he was standing in front of several other soldiers.

"You're wrong, Private," Reno replied quietly. "Goes for you and every soldier who comes into this town. Behave yourself and you won't have any trouble. Do something that's against the law, and you'll have me to reckon with."

"I ain't so sure that'd be a big chore," the soldier said, glancing about.

"Expect it would turn out to be more than you could handle," Magatagan said in a cool voice.

Crossing slowly to where the private and his friends were standing, Reno smiled bleakly.

"Just so you won't be forgetting," he said, and moving swiftly he swung the .44 still in his hand and clubbed the private solidly on the side of the head.

The soldier yelled in pain and surprise, staggered back, and sank into a chair. The men with him surged forward, shouting and cursing.

Magatagan waved them back with his weapon. "Settle down," he warned softly. "Never have liked it much when the odds were against me. You try rushing me and I'll forget making a club out of my gun and use the bullets."

The soldiers hesitated, and then all but one, a corporal, resumed their original positions. The noncom, arms folded across his chest, uniform in little better condition than that being worn by the private, stared at Magatagan coldly.

"Best you not try that, Marshal—if that's what you are, 'cause I sure don't see no star," he said. "You plug just one man from the post, and you'll have the whole garrison down on you. They'll tear this two-bit town apart."

"Soldier or not, any man who breaks the law answers for it. If he gets shot bucking me, it'll be his hard luck."

"Be yours, too—"

"Doubt that. I aim to have a talk with your commanding officer, warn him that he'd better keep you jaspers in line when you're in town or—"

The corporal laughed. "Be wasting your breath. The major don't give a tinker's damn what we do just so we show up for reveille. He figures, like us, this town's army property and we can all do what we damn please."

Jed Bleeker was no longer beside Rand, who had moved up and was behind the bar with Pete. Also, Dolly Jo was now in evidence, being with two other of the women at the balcony railing of the upper floor. Glancing over his shoulder, Reno backed slowly until his shoulders were against the wall adjacent to the salon's front entrance. The change provided him with an unimpeded view of the Bull's Head interior and eliminated the possibility of Bleeker or anyone else coming at him from behind.

"Best you forget that idea. It sure won't be that way as long as I'm marshal here," Magatagan said. "Want to make myself clear once more. I'm ordering all gunhands to leave town by morning—along with any other man who don't aim to live by the rules. Everybody else is welcome to stay. It's that simple— obey the law and you won't have any trouble; break it and you'll answer to me.

"Goes for every man jack at the fort, too, Corporal. Pass the word along when you get back, but I'll be having a talk with the major anyway."

"Can bet your bottom dollar I'll pass it along," the soldier said with a smirk. "And I sure can't wait to see what'll happen around here after I do."

Magatagan gave that subtle warning a bit of thought and then shrugged.

"I'm not one to chew my tobacco twice, Corporal, but you better tell plain what they'll be up against if they get out of line. And you can say that I'd as soon any man thinking on breaking the law would choose to fight me. That'd give me leave to kill him before he disturbed the peace or whatever he aimed to do."

The soldier, evidently chilled by the cold, matter-of-fact declaration, had no reply. Magatagan let his glance drift slowly about the saloon as he searched for further opposition. Monty Rand's features were expressionless, as were those of all others in the Bull's Head.

"I reckon I've made myself plenty clear," Reno said after a long breath of silence, and raising his eyes to Dolly Jo, he nodded slightly, wheeled, and stepped out onto the saloon's porch.

Again he felt the tautness that had gripped him earlier, but as before, it was an old, familiar sensation and he did not dislike it, for it gave him a feeling of high excitement, of a willingness to meet and cope with whatever might present itself.

Magatagan was too well acquainted with his own kind to think they would accept his ultimatum and depart the settlement. Some would, of course, convinced that continued living in the town was not worth the possibility of losing in a shoot-out; but there would be those overburdened with pride who would consider it a disgrace and a mark of cowardice to leave, and so elect to remain. He would deal with them when the proper time came.

Looking up and down the street, Reno had the urge to step out boldly into the driving sunlight and make an end-to-end tour of the settlement, thus showing his disdain for any who might be inclined to take a potshot at him. But that would be pressing his luck too far; only a damn fool would expose himself after laying down the law as he had.

But he reckoned a good lawman, endeavoring to firmly establish his authority, would not hide either. Holstering his weapon, swiping at the sweat beading his forehead with the back of a hand, Reno moved out onto the board sidewalk and, walking in a firm, square-shouldered way, started for his office.

☆ **16** ☆

Magatagan encountered a half-dozen or so Lynchburg residents during the short walk to his quarters, all of whom nodded or spoke cordially, if somewhat restrainedly. The fact that he was not wearing the marshal's star was of no import to them; as in the case of all small settlements, word of there being a new lawman had spread fast.

Entering his office, Reno found it had been dusted and swept, just as Lige Crow had promised, and his gear, including that which he'd left in his room at the Posada, was laid out on one of the benches. He'd remember to thank the stableman for collecting his belongings at the hotel, which he himself had intended to do. It was a gesture of kindness on Crow's part, one that indicated the willingness of the townspeople to make things as easy as possible for him.

Moving his gear into the adjoining living quarters, Reno tossed his blanket roll on the bed, emptied the saddlebags, stored what extra clothing he owned in the wardrobe, and placed what remained of his trail grub on the shelf behind the stove, along with his frying pan, lard tin, and cup.

He was pleased he'd not be doing any cooking—other than boiling up a pot of coffee now and then; a man got plenty tired of his own fixings when he was on the move, and it would be a real pleasure to make the most of Perkins' Restaurant while he was in Lynchburg. He'd noticed that he was all but out of coffee beans and needed to provide himself with a fresh supply. He'd drop by Broome's and pick up a sack— of the already-ground kind, this time.

A new bucket was in the tin sink built into a cabinet against one wall, and wondering about a water supply, Reno stepped to the window and looked out. The pump, mounted at the head of a trough, was but a short distance from the back door. And not far from it was a stack of wood, split and cut to proper size for the stove. Everything was arranged to be most convenient, Magatagan thought, which could mean the town went out of its way to keep its lawman satisfied.

Coming about, he returned to the street and, crossing over, made his way to Broome's. Mounting the steps, Reno crossed the square of landing, ordinarily used by merchants for displaying their wares but now conspicuously bare. He opened the screen door and entered. Lige Crow shouted a welcome to him from the rear of the store. At the same moment Broome also called out.

" 'Morning, Marshal," the storekeeper said. "I hear you've been right busy."

Magatagan, pausing briefly to let his eyes adjust from the bright sunlight to the darker interior of the building, nodded.

"Always figured it was smart to get in the first lick," he said, and continued on to where the two men stood.

"And you sure done that!" Crow said enthusiastically. "Was there in the Bull's Head when you told them soldiers and them toughs how the cow ate the cabbage! Was sure something to see—and hear!''

Broome was not smiling. Arms folded over the bib of his denim apron, he watched while Magatagan rolled a cigarette and then shook his head doubtfully.

"Not so sure your jumping them soldiers like you did was smart—''

Match in midair, Reno hesitated in lighting his smoke. His lips tightened slightly. Opposition to his methods already! He had expected to encounter some, but not so quickly—and certainly not from John Broome. Touching the small flame to the tip of the cylinder of tobacco, he puffed it into life and put his attention on the store owner.

"Soldiers or not, it makes no difference to me. They're going to respect the law same as everybody else. It just happened they were first in line for a lesson.''

"And them jaybirds sure got one,'' Crow exulted. "I'm betting that sergeant's head's still ringing!''

Broome's sober mien did not break. "I can understand the way you're looking at it, but we have to get along with the army best we can, and that could stir up trouble—''

"Now, hold on there, John!'' Crow broke in. "The deal was the marshal was to have a free hand if he took the job—and right off you're wanting to hamstring him. Let him be! I got a hunch he knows what he's doing.''

Broome frowned, shrugged. "Yes, I reckon so. It's only that the army—''

"I'll be riding out to the fort and having a talk with whoever's in command—a major—''

"Wagner—Bart Wagner,'' Crow supplied when

Reno hesitated. "Don't figure on getting much help out of him. He's about as nothing as a man can get."

"Now, he's not all that bad, Lige," Broome said, shaking his head. "Can't say as he's any great shakes as a post commander—soldiers all do pretty much as they please,—but while Powell's away—"

"Hell, that Wagner ain't worth spitting on," Crow declared. "Was they to ask me, that Captain Agnew would make a hell of a lot better headman—"

"No doubt, but Wagner outranks him, so he's the one in command, and there's nothing we can do about it."

The storekeeper paused, thoughtfully eyed Magatagan, who was standing by, lean features reflecting slight amusement as he sucked on his cigarette.

"What do you aim to say to Wagner?"

Reno's shoulders stirred indifferently. "Haven't made up any special speech other than telling him his men will have to behave when they're in town. Maybe'll think of something else by the time I get there. . . . Grind me up a pound of coffee beans, will you? Seems I'm out."

Broome turned without further comment, and taking a generous scoop of the brown beans from a glass container, something considerably more than the specified amount, he dumped them into the hopper of the grinder and began to crank the wheel.

"I reckon you found all your duds and things," Crow said. "Picked them up at the hotel when I got your horse."

"I did—and I'm obliged to you, Lige," Magatagan said as Broome funneled the ground coffee into a cloth sack. "I owe you anything?"

"Nothing a'tall," Crow said. "You'll be needing

your animal to ride out to the fort. Leaving pretty soon?''

"Pretty soon," Reno replied.

"Then I reckon I best get over to the barn and saddle him up," the stableman said, starting for the door. "Be seeing the both of you later."

Magatagan responded, but Broome, tying a bit of twine string around the neck of the sack containing the coffee, remained silent. Coming back around the counter, he handed it to Reno and waved off Magatagan's attempt to pay.

"Forget it," he said, "and forget what I was saying. Lige's right. You know what you're doing, and we give you a free hand to do it."

Magatagan smiled. "I won't get you into any trouble that I can't get you out of," he said, moving for the door. "Never was any hand to start something I couldn't finish. Obliged to you for the coffee."

Broome made a reply, inaudible to Reno as he pushed open the screen door and was once again in the driving sunlight. Pausing for a moment to sweep the street with his glance, he then crossed the landing and stepped down into the loose dust.

Midway to his office Magatagan slowed, a loud shout from a passageway lying between two buildings just ahead claiming his attention. Moving on until he was abreast of the corridor, he halted. Two soldiers, each with a bottle of whiskey and both on the verge of falling-down drunk, stared back at him, a foolish expression on their slack features.

The pair was bothering no one, and like as not, both would soon fall into a drunken slumber. Magatagan started to continue on his way, deciding to simply allow the liquor to have its quieting effect, and then an idea came to him: throwing them in jail would lend emphasis to not only the words he had spoken earlier in the Bull's Head, but also to what he would say later on when he talked to the commander out at Fort Shafter. Besides, the soldiers would be safer locked in the jail, where they could sleep off the whiskey unmolested.

Thrusting the sack of coffee inside his shirt to free both hands, Reno got the protesting men onto their feet and half-dragged, half-carried them to the jail, where he put them in separate cells.

"You taking my bottle?" one demanded in a thick voice.

Magatagan considered both glass containers. They were all but empty. "Finish them off—then get some sleep," he answered. "I'll turn you loose tomorrow."

"Sure, Sarge," the soldier mumbled, and stretched out on the bunk. "Sure am a-thanking you."

Magatagan grinned, checked the locks on both cells as well as that on the main door. The jail was secure. Pivoting, he started again for his office, quickening his step as a wave of pleasure surged through him. Lucilla Roth was standing in the doorway, smiling as she watched him approach.

☆ **17** ☆

A ghost from his childhood training pushed to the fore in Reno Magatagan's mind, and removing his hat, he nodded politely to the woman.

"A pleasure to see you, Lucilla."

She smiled brightly and stepped back, allowing him to enter the office. She had a basket filled with grocery items, and it was evident she had been doing her marketing for the night's supper.

"I was just passing," she said as he tossed the sack of coffee onto the rolltop, "and thought I'd stop by and remind you of tonight."

"No chance of me forgetting it," Magatagan said.

"Well, I know you're busy—and I just wanted to be sure," Lucilla said, and then added, "I just watched you put those two drunk soldiers in jail. You don't know how good it is to see someone upholding the law here in Lynchburg again. But won't you have trouble with the army—arresting a soldier?"

Reno shrugged as he studied the woman covertly. She was wearing a light-blue dress trimmed with narrow white lace. A small sunbonnet worn on the back of her head concealed most of her dark hair. Her eyes seemed bluer to him now, and he hadn't noticed before how full her brows were or how perfectly shaped were her lips. How would it feel to have a woman like her for a wife, he wondered? She looked to be, in every way, the answer to a man's fondest dreams.

"Could be, but it'll work out. Law applies to everybody—just happens that a couple of soldiers got caught breaking it first."

"First—after those in the saloon—"

Magatagan's shoulders stirred once again. "News sure gets around fast . . ."

"That's true," Lucilla said. "Hardly anything goes on that the whole town doesn't know about it in a couple of hours. . . . Well, I must hurry home, get my supper started. I'll be expecting you around six o'clock, if that's all right."

"Be fine," Reno said, and watched her turn, move off through the doorway into the street.

He stood motionless inside the office, now filling with the day's steadily rising heat, enjoying the faint odor of her perfume and the sight of her erect, graceful figure until his view was blocked by an intervening building.

Sighing deeply to relieve the frustration he felt, Reno picked up the sack of coffee, carried it into the adjoining room, and laid it on the shelf beside the tin he used as a coffeepot. He gave brief thought to boiling up a cup or two, but dismissed the idea; it would mean building a fire, and it was too hot for that. It would be easier to visit Phil Perkins' Restaurant, but that didn't appeal to him either, and now unaccountably restless, he went back into his office and stepped outside.

Not long after noon, he figured, glancing at the sun. As well ride out to Fort Shafter and have his understanding with Wagner, get that done and behind him. Anything was better than just sitting around, he decided, and started for the livery stable.

Crow was not there, but true to his word, the stableman had the bay saddled, bridled, and waiting in the first stall along the runway. Greeting the young boy who apparently was doing hostler duties, Magatagan asked directions to the fort, got them from the youngster, and mounting up, quickly loped the short distance to the encampment.

Fort Shafter was in a surprisingly poor and neglected condition, Reno noted as he rode through the unattended gate and halted. Several uniformed men loafing in the shade fronting the enlisted men's barracks glanced up. At once their gullied faces hardened. They had no doubt heard of what had taken place earlier in the Bull's Head, he reckoned—or possibly had even been there. It was doubtful they knew anything yet about the pair he'd jailed for drunkenness.

"Where'll I find the commanding officer?" he asked, returning their hostile stares with equal chill.

One of the soldiers jerked a thumb at the building on the opposite side of the bleak parade ground.

"Upstairs—"

Magatagan said, "Obliged," and then added, "Want to talk to the provo, too. He around?"

"We ain't no goddamn information bureau," one of the group began angrily, and abruptly fell silent when the man next him laid a cautioning hand on his arm.

"What'll you be wanting to tell him?"

"Personal business. When you see him, say I'm looking for him," Reno said coolly, and rode on.

Halting at the hitch rack erected at the end of the long building, Magatagan dropped back to the board sidewalk, and aware now of the dozen or more soldiers who had come into the open since his arrival, he made his way to its entrance and turned in. There was a curious lack of activity at the post—no drilling, no moving about, no work details, not even any horses anywhere in sight, although the unmistakable smell of stables was strong on the hot air.

Climbing the stairway before him, Reno went up to the second level and, crossing a small landing, entered the office above which was the sign: POST COMMANDER. Except for a man dozing in a chair behind a table, the room was empty. Magatagan stepped up to the table, noting as he did the insignia of a major on the officer's shoulders. This would be Bart Wagner, he concluded, and rapped sharply on the table.

Wagner, a narrow-faced, sly-eyed man, came bolt upright in his chair. He stared blankly at Magatagan and then flung an angry glance at a second desk on the opposite side of the room.

"Where the hell's that goddamn dog robber? Supposed to be on duty," he shouted, and then placed his wrathful attention on Reno. "Who the devil are you—and what do you want?"

"Name's Magatagan. I'm the new town marshal—"

"Marshal!" Wagner echoed loudly, and then frowned darkly. "Heard about you slapping some of my men around."

"Just one," Reno corrected. "Reason I'm here. There'll be more getting the same treatment and then going to jail if they don't mind their manners when they're in town."

"The hell!" Wagner yelled, coming to his feet. "Mister, we own that town. We'll do as we goddamn please!" A wild gleam filled the officer's eyes, and his voice had risen almost to a hysterical level. "You hear me?"

"I hear, but that's not the way it's going to be," Reno said quietly. "I've been hired to keep the peace, and I aim to do it. Soldiers are no exception."

"That lousy stink hole's on a military reservation, and that puts it under army jurisdiction—"

"Maybe. Nobody knows for sure that's true, and until your colonel gets back, we'll figure it's not. Means I'll enforce the law inside the town's limits. Want you to pass that word along to your men—"

"I will like hell!" Wagner stormed, sweat glistening on his face. "You're not the law, Magatagan, or whatever they call you, and any the town needs I'll supply."

Reno, maintaining a firm grip on his temper, shook his head. "No, Major, you best forget that. Town needs but one lawman—and I'm him. You run the fort, I'll run the town."

The color of Wagner's complexion deepened as his rage increased. Abruptly he made a gesture at the open doorway.

"Get—get the hell out of here!" he stammered. "Else I'll have you thrown in the guardhouse for— for trespassing on army premises! And don't you ever show up around here ag'in—or I'll do just that!"

"I don't expect to be back," Magatagan said. "Only reason I came this time was serve notice on you and the men garrisoned here how things will be in town from now on. If you're smart, you'll pass the word to them."

"By God, I'll declare the damn place off limits—"

"No, they're welcome there as long as they behave."

"You're goddamn right they are—and they'll keep going there if and when they want."

Magatagan, impatience now replacing his own anger, wheeled and started for the door. "Had my say. Rest is up to you," he stated over a shoulder, and returning to the stairs, he descended and retraced his steps along the walk to his horse.

Swinging into the saddle, he rode past the saluting cannon and lonely flagpole, and on across the empty parade, wondering again at the deserted, uncared-for look of the post. The cluster of men in front of the barracks had doubled, he noticed as he drew the bay to a stop before them.

"The provo?" he said questioningly.

One of the soldiers shook his head. "Ain't around, and I don't know where the bast—he is. Maybe down on the creek fishing."

"Or vis'ting that little Mex gal he's been—"

The soldier's words ended suddenly as the dull thud of horses approaching the gate drew everyone's attention. Reno shifted his eyes. A sergeant—big, heavy, round face and neck red from the heat—appeared in the opening. Behind him, horse at the end of a short lead rope, was a young boy—a prisoner, to judge from his bound hands.

"What's the sarge up to?" one of the men wondered, rising and moving toward the noncom and his charge. "The kid one of our bunch?"

"Don't recollect him. Must belong to Company C," the man next to him said. "Whatever, he's getting took to the guardhouse, and that sure ain't no fun these hot days."

Magatagan watched the pair ride by. Likely the boy was a deserter or perhaps he had just committed some other infraction of army regulations—which

Reno knew were only too numerous if there was an overly zealous officer around.

Lifting the reins, Magatagan touched the bay with his spurs and moved on. Since it seemed the provost marshal was not to be found, he had no further business at the fort. His thought had been to talk to the soldier bearing such authority along the lines followed with Major Bart Wagner, and try and enlist his cooperation. He'd see if he could get in touch with the man later, Reno decided, and put the bay to a lope.

Magatagan, finding time heavy on his hands after returning from the fort, prepared himself for the evening with Lucilla Roth by purchasing a new shirt and pair of pants from Broome's, and further spruced up his appearance by shaving again.

Such took only a couple of the hours that intervened before he was to present himself at the dressmaker's, and to make use of them, he walked the town to familiarize himself with the buildings, both occupied and vacant, the passageways that lay between, and all other pertinent information that could be of help in the future.

A curious hush hung over the settlement, one that he could not help but notice. It was as if everyone, including the outlaw faction, was standing back waiting to see if something out of the ordinary was going to happen. It was so pronounced that Reno half-expected to encounter some of Monty Rand's bunch as he prowled about, but not once in all the time he spent circulating around did he see any of them.

Nor did he chance upon any soldiers from the fort; and that, combined with the absence of Rand's hard cases on the street, struck him as odd. But his thoughts were so centered on Lucilla Roth and the evening he would be spending with her that he gave the matter only passing consideration.

Six o'clock finally came, and prompt to the minute, Magatagan knocked on the door of the woman's small cottage at the rear of her shop. Lucilla responded immediately, standing before him in the fading light of day, tall, cool in a figure-revealing dress of soft gray with leg-of-mutton sleeves, dark hair gathered about her face and arranged loosely on the nape of her neck, pale-blue eyes filled with welcome.

"I hope it's not too warm in here for you," she said, stepping aside that he might enter. "I've opened the back door and all of the windows to create a draft, but it doesn't seem to have done much good. The cooking—"

"Feels fine in here," Magatagan said, dismissing her apology as he halted in the center of the small parlor and glanced about.

It was a cozy, comfortable room laden at the moment with the enticing odors of the supper Lucilla had prepared. At that moment Abby appeared, starched-looking in a beribboned white dress. She greeted Reno with a big smile, paused long enough to thank him again for what he'd done for her, and then disappeared into the rear of the house.

The supper, served in an adjoining room, consisted of beef roast so tender it could be cut with a fork; potatoes, onions, and other vegetables cooked to mealiness; warm light bread; honey; and the hot apple pie coated with fresh butter, and black coffee. It all made for a meal such as Reno Magatagan had not enjoyed since he was a youngster in the family home.

When it was over, he and Lucilla returned to the

parlor while Abby, insisting on it, took care of clearing the table and seeing to the dishes.

"Sure want to tell you what a treat that was," Reno said as they each sat down in the heavy, chintz-covered rocking chairs. "Man on the move never gets the chance at a meal like that."

"Thank you," Lucilla replied. "I thought of having steak with fried potatoes and such, then I realized you probably had them quite often. I was hoping you'd like the change."

"Couldn't have been better," Magatagan said, taking out his cigarette makings. "It all right if I smoke?"

"Of course—I enjoy the smell of tobacco," Lucilla said. "How did your meeting with Major Wagner go?"

Reno, busy rolling his cigarette, smiled wryly. "Can't say there was much use going out there and talking to him. He didn't take kindly to what I had to say at all."

"I doubted that he would—"

Magatagan thrust the thin cylinder of tobacco between his lips and lit it. "You know him?" he asked after exhaling a small cloud of smoke.

"Some. I won't say that I consider him a friend."

"Probably goes for everybody else around here if he's always like he was today. Fort sure looks bad—rundown, I mean. And what soldiers I saw were just laying around, doing nothing."

"That's the way it's been all along, I've been told. But I guess it's even worse with Colonel Powell gone."

"Been in a few forts in my life, don't think I ever saw one where discipline had gone to hell—was missing like it is out there."

"Which won't make your job as marshal any easier,'' Lucilla said. ''There are times when the soldiers come to town and really get out of hand.'' The woman paused as a crash sounded in the kitchen, where Abby was washing the dishes. She smiled wryly and continued, ''I expect you have done a great deal of traveling.''

''About all I have done since I grew up—''

''Were you just, well—drifting?'' There was a faint disapproval in Lucilla Roth's tone, as if, like most women, she saw no value in aimless wandering.

''Can't say it was exactly like that,'' Reno said, studying the tip of his cigarette. ''I was looking for a man.'' He hesitated, and then added bluntly, ''To kill him.''

Lucilla dropped her gaze. ''Did you find him?''

''Yes. He was the one I mentioned to you all when you asked me to take on the job as your town marshal.''

The woman was quiet for several moments and then, sighing, said, ''I'm sure you had good reason, if you spent so many years searching for him.''

Reno gave that thought, debating with himself the wisdom and need of revealing what had been his life for so long. He concluded Lucilla might as well know the truth about him. Not that he could expect it to lead to anything—he would be gone in a few more days, most likely probably to never see the woman again—but for some reason he felt he would like her to know.

''My pa was an outlaw,'' he said, coming out flatly with it. ''First lived in Kentucky. He was a farmer there, but we couldn't make it, so the family— him, my ma, younger brother, and me—picked up and moved to Kansas.

''Turned out things were no better there, so Pa

threw in with a man he got acquainted with named Henry Bigbee. Bigbee was a small-time crook, and he and Pa decided to get into it right—robbing banks, stagecoaches carrying payrolls, and the like.''

Magatagan's cigarette had gone out. He paused to relight it, his dark eyes on the woman as he sought to assess her reaction to what he was saying. In that, he had failed so far; Lucilla's smooth features were calm, expressionless.

''They never did come out with much,'' he continued, ''but Ma managed to keep the family going with what little cash Pa gave her. Times were hard and nobody had any money to speak of—even the ones who had jobs—so we just sort of rocked along, living from day to day. I know I never thought much about how we lived. Schooling and chores were taking up most of my time.

''Then Pa and Bigbee got word of a big gold shipment that was going to be made. They made plans, ambushed the stage, and got the money. But when they were getting away, Pa's horse got shot out from under him. Bigbee could have given him a hand—he had plenty of time—but he saw the chance to keep all the gold for himself, so he rode on and left Pa there for the law to grab.

''Pa was sent to the pen, died there after a while. Just couldn't live cooped up, I guess. Bigbee just disappeared. Ma took it real hard. She made me swear, before she died, that I'd hunt Bigbee down and make him pay—kill him—for what he'd done to our family. Just what I did.''

''You said something about a brother. Didn't he—''

''He died not long after we moved to Kansas. Was always kind of sickly. . . . It took a pile of years to find Bigbee. He'd changed his name to Locklear, but

I finally tracked him down and squared things for Ma and Pa. It was a fair fight—I gave him his chance; then, when it was done, I headed down this way, figuring to hang up my gun and start a new life for myself someday.''

''I still don't understand. If it was a fair fight, why do you have to run?''

Magatagan shrugged, rose, and opening the door of the small heating stove set in a corner of the room, tossed the butt of his lifeless cigarette into it. All was quiet in the kitchen now, an indication that Abby had finished her chores and was elsewhere in the house.

''Had a few set-tos with the law during the time I was hunting Bigbee, and they don't look upon me as an upstanding citizen. Fair fight or not, I knew they'd come looking for me. It's been that way all along— like I said, a man gets a reputation and the law never forgets him.''

''I think I see what you're up against,'' Lucilla said, smoothing the folds of her dress where it puckered in her lap. ''I only hope you—''

There was a knock at the door. Lucilla hesitated, then got to her feet and crossed to the entry. Reno heard her in low conversation for several minutes, and then looked up as she returned. Her face was drawn with concern. At once Magatagan rose.

''Something gone wrong?''

''Terribly,'' the woman, close to tears, replied. ''That was a neighbor of mine. He said that Danny Stark—he's the boy that Abby's going to marry—had been arrested this morning by the army and taken to the fort.''

A flash of remembrance came to Magatagan; the young man he'd seen the sergeant bringing into the post just as he was riding out. The prisoner must have been Stark.

"Your neighbor say why the army had picked him up?"

Lucilla nodded. Her voice was strained when she replied. "They claim he robbed and—and assaulted some woman. She complained to a soldier friend of hers, and he called in the army, I guess. I—I just can't believe it! Danny's just not that kind of boy!"

Lucilla turned abruptly to Reno. He took her into his arms, comforted her as best he could.

"I—I don't know how to tell Abby," she murmured, her voice low and desperate.

"No way out of it," Magatagan said. "Something I aim to look into, though. The army's overstepping itself, picking up the boy off the compound. Was my job as town marshal. I'll ride out there again in the morning and have a talk with that major."

"I'll talk to him too," Lucilla said, drawing back slightly to dab at her eyes. "He'll probably drop by here."

Reno looked closely at her. "Then he's more than just somebody you know?"

"He'd like to be, but I'm in no way interested."

Magatagan's stiff frame eased a bit. Again he drew her into his arms and held her close. Then, "Leave everything to me—let me see what I can do about it." Releasing the woman, he turned to get his hat. "Don't worry too much if you can help it, but I know how much he means to you and your daughter, so I know that's asking a lot. Now, I'll do everything I can for him," he added, moving for the door. "Sure want to thank you again for the fine supper. . . . Good night."

"Good night," Lucilla responded as he stepped out into the night.

                    *   *   *

Bart Wagner, standing in the deep shadows of the lilac bushes a few steps from the entrance to Lucilla Roth's house, drew back farther into the darkness as Magatagan emerged.

A jealous anger was surging through the officer. He had watched the two embrace, had heard the low murmur of their voices, although the words spoken had been inaudible. But he could imagine their meaning.

Wagner had been outside the cottage for some time, holding back his intended visit to Lucilla, during which he planned to tell her of Danny Stark's arrest while emphasizing the seriousness of the charges the boy faced; but when he arrived, he'd seen Magatagan there in the parlor with her. Shortly after that, someone, a friend of Lucilla's, had come and relayed the news of the boy's arrest.

Everything had worked out wrong for him, Wagner thought angrily. He had wanted to be the one who told the woman about Stark's arrest so that he could make a point of offering to help. But that was lost now. Too, that goddamn town marshal was in on it, but he guessed he could handle that.

No doubt the so-called lawman would show up bright and early at post headquarters in the morning, demanding to know by what right had the army picked up the boy. Well, he'd damn quick be reminded that the town was on a military reservation and the army had every right.

That ought to settle the question of authority once and for all as far as Magatagan was concerned, and it should get him out of the picture if he and Lucilla had something going between them. When she learned that the marshal couldn't help her, but that he could, she'd change her tune mighty quick.

Moving out of the deeper shadows where he could again look into the front room of the house, Walker saw that Lucilla was no longer in the parlor, was apparently elsewhere—most likely comforting the girl.

He'd forget talking to her now, wait until morning. By then Lucilla would have had a chance to do a lot of thinking, and worrying—all of which would make matters easier for him.

☆ **19** ☆

As could be expected, Abby took the news of
Danny Stark's arrest and imprisonment very hard.
Lucilla, too, had slept fitfully. She was up early,
dressed, and had only coffee for breakfast while she
made plans for the day. She'd get a horse and buggy
from the livery stable and drive out to Fort Shafter,
and there appeal to Bart Wagner on behalf of Danny—
that would be the first thing to do.

She wasn't sure how much good it would do—none
at all, possibly—but for Abby's sake she had to try.
Too, Reno Magatagan had said he'd call on Major
Wagner for the same purpose. Perhaps, between them,
they could get something done for the boy. Of course,
if he was guilty of the things the woman, whoever
she was, had claimed, it would be difficult for anyone to help him.

But Lucilla wasn't convinced that Danny was capable of the crimes of which he was being accused.
He simply wasn't that kind of a person, being one
who never drank or smoked, never helled around, as
the saying went, but was serious and hardworking,
and was looking forward to marrying Abby.

Things did happen to people, Lucilla had to admit—
times when circumstances prompted them to do things
utterly unexpected of them—and such could have

been the case with Danny. She could not believe that, though; for Abby's sake she'd never admit openly that such was possible. And in reality she herself doubted the possibility.

Maybe it would be better to call on the woman who had lodged the charges against Danny. She didn't know who she was, of course—someone who lived there in town, Lucilla guessed. Bart Wagner could supply that information. She'd make a point of finding out the woman's name and where she lived when she talked to the army officer.

Lucilla turned her attention to the door. Someone had knocked. Setting her near-empty cup aside, she rose to answer the summons. One of Abby's friends, she supposed, come to extend what comfort she could to the distraught girl. Opening the panel, Lucilla was surprised. It was Bart Wagner.

"Good morning. I know it's early," he said. "But I thought we should have a talk as soon as possible—considering what has happened to the Stark boy."

Lucilla reached up, unhooked the screen door, and pushed it open. She was mystified as to why the officer would take such interest in the matter—so much so that he would call upon her almost before breakfast. Unless . . . A furrow crossed Lucilla's brow as a thought came to her mind. Unless he was there for another reason.

"Want to say that I'm sorry this has happened to the boy. I know how important he is to you, getting married to your daughter and all that. It's a real shame that he had to go and get himself in such serious trouble."

A faint sigh of relief slipped from Lucilla's lips. She had feared that Bart Wagner was there to press her again for an acceptance of his proposal. She had figured him wrong; he seemed genuinely interested in Danny Stark's troubles. She smiled, motioned at the adjoining room.

"I have some fresh coffee made. If you'd care for a cup—"

"Thanks, no—had my meal early this morning. Felt it was most important that I see you first thing. Lucilla, that boy's in mighty serious trouble." Lucilla indicated one of the rockers with an offhand gesture and sank into the other. Although she disliked the idea, she would be civil to Wagner—just in hopes he could do something for Danny.

"You don't think he's guilty, do you?" she asked.

"Not for me to say," the officer replied in a crisp, businesslike manner. "I'll have to leave that to a military court. I must say, however, that the evidence is strong against him."

"Is there any evidence, or is it just the word of this woman—whoever she is?"

"She told my sergeant that her daughter was there in the house at the time and saw it all. Naturally the girl will be called as a witness."

Lucilla brushed nervously at her mouth. "I still won't believe it. I'd like to talk to the woman."

"I doubt if that would be possible—you being so close to the boy—"

"What difference does that make? Don't I have the right to do all I can for Danny?"

"The court might think you were trying to scare off the woman—intimidate her."

Lucilla laughed, the sound harsh and brittle and unlike her. "They'd be right! Truth is, I'll even buy her off. I'm willing to turn over everything I have— my house, my furniture, even my dressmaker's shop— to her if she'll forget the charges and let Danny go free so that he and Abby can have a life of their own.''

Wagner scrubbed at his smooth chin. "Maybe there *is* a way," he said thoughtfully. Outside, in a nearby cottonwood, a thrasher had broken into song and was filling the early-morning quiet with his music.

Lucilla leaned forward hopefully. "There is?" she pressed anxiously. "Do you really think so?"

He nodded. "Happens I'm post commander while Powell's away. Big advantage in that. I could—maybe—have the charges against the boy dropped for—say, lack of firm evidence."

"Oh, Bart . . . could you? I'd be ever so grate-ful—"

"No reason that I couldn't that I can think of, except—"

"Except what?"

"Well, let's be practical, and say that it really comes down to you and me. After all, I'm only human, and you're the most desirable woman I've ever met. Now, you only have to—"

As Wagner paused, his eyes bold and unyielding, Lucilla felt a wave of anger and despair rush through her. His meaning was only too clear.

"What you're saying is that if I'll consent to being your private woman—your barracks wife—you'll ar-range for Danny to go free."

"A bit crudely put, but that about covers it."

Lucilla was silent. The thrasher was no longer singing in the nearby tree, having moved on for some reason, leaving a sort of emptiness that matched her sinking spirits.

"I don't need to remind you again of the advan-tages you would have," Wagner said. "Mentioned them before, but mostly you'd have an easy life,

your daughter would be happily married and no longer
a source of worry to you. And I'm a gentle man—I'd
be good to you.''

Lucilla raised her eyes and looked at the officer. It
wouldn't be too bad, she supposed. He was clean,
well-off, was a man of authority at the fort, and
while his face was a bit too narrow to be handsome
and his eyes contained a deep slyness, she no doubt
could do worse. Do worse! Lucilla chided herself
sharply. She was looking at it as if Wagner was
proposing marriage! All he was offering was a back-
alley life as his private doxie!

But again, maybe it wouldn't be too bad. She was
no wide-eyed schoolgirl filled with dreams of pure
love and looking for an exciting, wonderful life. She
had already been on that road and knew the truth—
that reality was a chain of heartaches, sacrifice, and
compromise.

Too, what else did the future hold for her? The
often dreary, always confining world of dressmaking,
in which she strove to please the women who conde-
scended to favor her with their patronage? An exis-
tence that provided nothing but monotony—and
advancing age?

That, and nothing more. There'd never be another
man like Reno Magatagan come along and arouse her
interest as had he, and a future with him, thanks to
what he admittedly was, could never be. Not that she
would object to that; he fascinated and stirred up
currents within her that made her tremble, and if
asked, she would go to the end of the world with
him. But that was out of the question—he had no
place for her in his scheme of things—as well forget
Reno Magatagan.

"I don't like to say it," Bart Wagner's words

pushed dully into her thoughts, "but what that boy is up against—an assault on a woman—means he'll go before a firing squad if the court finds him guilty, which I'm afraid it will."

"I understand," Lucilla said woodenly. "Either I agree to your terms or Danny will die. It's that simple."

Wagner shifted uncomfortably. His shoulders stirred. "I suppose you could boil it down to that, but it makes an arrangement between us sound cold-blooded and heartless. You could see it in another way—as, well, two people in love and getting together."

"Don't speak of love!" Lucilla snapped, coming to her feet. "Love will having nothing to do with it—and you know that! An arrangement, that's all it will be."

Wagner came upright also. Picking up his hat from the table, he faced her. "Look at it however you please," he said coolly. "I'm only trying to put it in the best light. But I must warn you, Lucilla—I need your answer by noon today; otherwise, it will be too late to do anything for the boy."

She nodded lifelessly. "You'll have it."

Magatagan, sitting near a window in Phil Perkin's Restaurant, straightened slowly when he saw Major Bart Wagner, in company with three soldiers, ride in. They drew up in the center of the street, conversed briefly, and then separated, the enlisted men pointing straight for the Bull's Head, Wagner coming about and moving off into an opposite direction.

Reno's frown deepened when he saw the officer pull into the hitching rack near Lucilla Roth's dressmaking shop, dismount, secure his horse, and then walk briskly down the path that led to her cottage. He recalled that Lucilla had said she was acquainted with Wagner, but indicated she didn't care for the man. The early call likely was not social, he realized moments later; the subject, knowing that Danny Stark was the intended husband of her daughter, Abby, had come to talk to Lucilla about him.

One thing, the officer coming to town would save him a ride out to the fort, Reno thought, finishing up his second cup of breakfast coffee. He'd catch Wagner after he left Lucilla's, and have a few words with him about the boy.

Rising, Magatagan nodded to Perkins, made his way to the doorway, and stepped out into the sunshine. Halting on the small board landing to roll a cigarette, Reno glanced along the street. The soldiers who had ridden in with Wagner had tethered their horses at the saloon's rack, were now on the Bull's Head porch, where several other men were lounging about.

Reno thought he recognized Jed Bleeker as one of the latter, guessed Monty Rand had followed instructions and was ridding himself of his hard-case hangers-on. He'd best keep an eye on the bunch, however, see that they did ride on. The soldiers would bear watching, too, as their presence there so early in the day could mean trouble.

Trouble . . . That reminded Reno of Danny Stark and the fix the boy had got himself into. He'd promised Lucilla to do what he could for Danny, which called for, first off, getting him out of the army's hands and under the town's authority, where he rightfully belonged and where he could await trial before a territorial judge. That was a matter he'd take up with Major Wagner just as soon as the officer left Lucilla Roth's.

Meanwhile, he'd make some inquries of his own concerning Danny Stark. Not knowing the boy at all, he could not be so certain of his innocence, as was Lucilla, and he knew only too well how easily a man could be misled by the opinions of others who, perhaps, were blinded by close friendship and loyalty. It would be better, if he was to help Danny, to get as much information on the boy as possible.

John Broome, at the general store, flatly stated that he did not believe Danny capable of such crimes. Ed Stone was equally vehement. Continuing on the livery stable, Magatagan brought the question up to Lige Crow.

"Yeh, was hearing about that last night," the

stableman said. "I'm giving you odds there ain't nothing to it."

"You know who the woman is?"

"Nope. Somebody said she was a friend of O'Hanlon's, the sergeant that collared the boy and took him out to the fort. Only thing that puzzles me, howsomever, is why the woman would make a claim like that against the boy, unless it is true."

Magatagan hadn't thought of it in that light. "Makes me wonder, too," he said. "Army wouldn't have anything against Stark—leastwise, I haven't heard of it." He hesitated. "Think I'd better have a talk with that sergeant, too. I was out at the fort yesterday when he rode in with the boy."

"That's something else that's got me guessing," Crow said. "I ain't never seen the army handle a deal like that the way they did this one. Usually send three or four men along when they go after some fellow. A dozen times or more I've seen them grab some yellowlegs who'd overstayed his leave at the saloon, and there was always a sergeant with maybe a whole squad to back him."

"Maybe they figured Danny, being not much more'n a kid, wouldn't take any body but the sergeant," Reno said, "but it's something I wouldn't know much about. Passed through a few forts in my time, and that's all."

Crow wagged his head. "Well, the whole blasted thing seems mighty funny to me. There's that major now, coming from down the street."

Reno pivoted, faced in the direction Lige had indicated. Wagner had just pulled away from the hitching rack.

"Want to talk to him—like for you to come along,"

Magatagan said, and started toward the officer. "Major!"

At the call Wagner slowed. A look of annoyance crossed his face when he recognized Magatagan. "Yes?"

"Like a word with you," Reno said, halting in front of the officer. Lige Crow had followed and was nearby. He had wanted the stable owner present as a witness to what would be said.

"I'm in a hurry," Wagner began, but Crow moved forward and grasped the bridle of the officer's horse in his big hand.

"I reckon what the marshal's got to say won't take long," he said, grinning affably.

Wagner's face, a light pink, as if he had just shaved, darkened perceptibly. "All right, all right—get on with it!"

"The boy you're holding on the post guardhouse—I want him," Magatagan stated flatly. "He's a civilian and has the right to be tried before a circuit judge."

"It's a military matter," Wagner snapped. "The crime occurred yesterday morning on army premises."

"Supposed to have happened right here in town, from what we've been told—and the town's not under your command."

"Far as I'm concerned it is!" Wagner declared in a rising voice.

"Not far as I'm concerned—and for sure not until your colonel gets back from Washington with their decision," Reno said quietly.

"And you sure didn't have no right to grab that boy," Crow pointed out hotly. "Was up to the marshal, not any of your goddamn soldiers!"

Wagner brushed at the sweat on his face and stared off in the direction of the Bull's Head. There were still several men gathered on its porch, but the soldiers were not among them, apparently having gone inside, as their horses were still in evidence. Somewhere back in the ragged row of houses behind the business buildings a dog barked and a child was crying.

"Matter of opinion," Wagner said, seemingly calm. "Regardless, the boy stays right where he is."

Magatagan's voice was equally firm and quiet. "No, he belongs in the town's jail. I'm asking you to turn him over to me. When the word gets out that you had your sergeant throw him in the fort's guardhouse for something he did—or was supposed to have done—here in town things could get out of hand."

Wagner smiled patronizingly. "Really?"

"You can bank on it. You—the army—haven't done much to get along with folks here—people who've sunk their money into businesses, and made their homes, and helped build the town—and they're not going to stand by and let you railroad Stark, or anybody else living here, without doing something to stop it."

"Can't see that there's much you or the town can do," Wagner said indifferently. "I've enough men garrisoned at Shafter to handle any civilian uprising and—"

"From what I saw yesterday, you probably couldn't muster a dozen ablebodied men to make a stand, but that's just what I don't want, Major—a shooting showdown between the army and the townspeople. Can sidestep it by turning Stark over to me for a trial before a civilian judge."

"Not a chance," the officer replied bluntly, and jerked his horse free of Lige Crow's grip. "He'll be brought up before a court of officers over which I'll be presiding, and if the evidence warrants his being found guilty, he'll be sentenced to death by a firing squad.''

Lige swore deeply. Magatagan, holding tight rein on his temper, shook his head and looked away.

"Not saying the evidence is all against Stark," Wagner continued in a condescending tone. "Could be he'll be released—but that's for the court to say. Meantime, best thing you can do, Marshal, is look after the drunks and stay out of matters that don't concern you.''

"Happens Danny Stark does," Reno said. "When's this military court going to try the boy?''

"Tomorrow morning," Wagner said, and abruptly pulling away, he struck off in the direction of the fort.

☆ **21** ☆

Reno watched the officer, sitting ramrod straight in his saddle, ride off. Crow hawked, spat into the dust.

"That Stark boy sure ain't liable to get a fair shake from that jasper—can bet on that!"

It was evident to Magatagan also, but he was still uncertain as to what could be done about it. Danny Stark should be brought up before a territorial judge—of that he was certain—but just how to bring it about without open warfare with Wagner and the soldiers at Fort Shafter was the question. Too, if the boy *was* guilty—and Reno had to admit he had not the slightest proof either way—what difference who punished Stark?

He, personally, had been on the wrong side of the law for so many years that he'd long since come to the conclusion that it didn't matter who meted out the punishment; it all had the same result.

"You done with me? I got some harness mending to do, and—"

Magatagan glanced at Crow. "Go ahead. I just wanted somebody from the town along to hear what Wagner would say in case things got real serious later on."

"Meaning?"

"Ain't sure what I mean, because I don't know

myself. One thing for damn sure, I'm not letting that boy go up before a military court unless I'm sure he's guilty.''

"How do you aim to find that out?" Crow asked as together they started back down the street.

"Going to have a talk with the sergeant I saw bringing Danny in—O'Hanlon. Want to do some talking with the woman Danny's supposed to've gotten mixed up with, too."

"O'Hanlon can tell you who she is. Heard somebody say she was a right close friend of his. . . . Now, if you need me again, you know where I'll be.''

"Obliged to you," Reno said, and continued on as the stable owner turned away.

Magatagan went first to the jail, and there released the two soldiers, now both drawn-faced and sober and suffering from the aftereffects of too much whiskey. They greeted him sullenly, but brightened considerably when he told them to go get their breakfasts— since it was now too late for mess call at the fort—at Phil Perkins' Restaurant, the cost of which he would cover.

They departed at once, and as he closed and locked the doors of the jail behind them, a hail from the street brought him around.

"Marshal! Want to talk to you!"

It was the rancher, Laymon. He spurred the buckskin he was riding in close and swung down. Anger sparked the big man's eyes, and his mouth was set to a grim line.

"What's this I'm hearing about the Stark boy being jugged by the army? Just been told about it."

"They've got him in the guardhouse for raping

and then robbing some woman," Magatagan said. "Aim to try him in the morning."

"And you're standing around letting them do it? Hell, you're the marshal here, and it was you that should've jailed him."

"Didn't know about it until they'd picked up the boy. Talked to Major Wagner—"

"Wagner, that son of a bitch!" Laymon exploded. "Might know he's at the bottom of it. Who's the woman?"

"Don't know yet, but I'm on my way to find out."

"I see. When was it they say the boy was with her? He's been on the job steady—"

"Was yesterday morning."

The rancher swore again. "Why, dammit, it's all a lie! The boy was busy all yesterday morning working calves for me. I've got a half a dozen men who'll swear to it!"

Magatagan had come to attention at the rancher's words. This could be the proof he needed that Danny Stark was innocent, that he was being framed by someone, for some reason.

"He was here in town when a sergeant from the fort picked him up—"

"That would've been around noon. I sent him in to see Ed Stone about some feed. By God! Somebody's trying to hang a ringer on that boy!"

"Looks like that to me," Magatagan agreed.

"Then what the hell are you aiming to do about it? You going to just stand around let Wagner and his kangaroo court hang it on Danny? Well, I ain't! I'll get a dozen of my riders together and go bust him out of that guardhouse. They've been spoiling for a fight with them damn—"

"Back off, Laymon!" Magatagan cut in sharply. "It may come to that, but we best try everything else first. Sure don't want any shooting if we can dodge it."

"Dodge it!" the rancher echoed, looking at Reno in surprise. "That's mighty strange coming from you—a man who's lived by his gun!"

"That's how it used to be," Magatagan said evenly, "but that's all behind me. I'm hoping I won't ever need to use my gun on a man again."

"You think you can bargain with that dressed-up popinjay Wagner? He won't listen—"

"Know that. Talked to him a bit ago and got nowhere, and it may come down to going out to the fort after the boy. But first I want to see if I can find out who it is that's trying to frame Danny."

"What difference will that make?" Laymon demanded impatiently.

"Plenty. If I can get to the bottom of it, I can stop Wagner, who seems mighty anxious to stand the boy up in front of a firing squad, before he goes any further."

Reno paused, considered the rancher quietly for several moments. Then, "I don't want this to get out of hand. Like your word that you won't try anything on your own, but will wait till I've got things squared away, and—"

"I ain't much for stalling around," Laymon broke in angrily. "When there's something that needs doing, I'm for doing it right then."

"Even if it gets some good men killed when it was uncalled for?"

The rancher shrugged. "Well, this ain't something that ought to be put off, but you're the marshal and I reckon I'll string along with you. What do you want me to do?''

"Go on back to your ranch while I do some digging around. Soon as I'm ready to make a move—if it turns out we'll have to—I'll send word to you. Come in then with as many of your men as you can. We'll want to make a big showing when we go to the fort.''

"Sounds right to me. Where'll we meet?'' Laymon said.

"Here at the jail—''

"Good,'' the rancher responded, and turning about, he stepped up into the saddle of his buckskin and headed out of town.

Magatagan heaved a sigh of relief and glanced again to the Bull's Head. There were now none of the hard cases in sight, all having ridden on as he had ordered, he hoped. If they were defying him, they'd be inside the saloon. He'd look into that possibility, but first he wanted to talk with Lucilla Roth.

As far as he was concerned, Laymon had the proof that Danny Stark was not guilty of the charges placed against him, and she should know that. Too, he was wondering about Bart Wagner—why the officer had paid a call so early on the woman. Moving out into the street, he walked quickly to her house.

She apparently saw him when he turned onto the path leading to the cottage, for she was standing in the doorway awaiting him. Her face was strained, and there was a lost, helpless look in her eyes when she spoke.

"I—I was hoping you'd come—''

Magatagan pulled off his hat as he stepped past her into the parlor. "Got a bit of good news I figured you'd like to hear.''

"I can certainly use it," Lucilla said, her tone bitter. "Just had a talk with Major Wagner."

"Saw him ride up, and leave—"

"He offered to let Danny go if I would become his woman," she continued, coming straight out with it.

Magatagan drew up stiffly. "Woman? You mean marry him—become his wife?"

"No. He's already got a wife back East somewhere. I'd be—"

Lucilla's voice broke as frustration swept through her. Reno, anger now tightening the corners of his jaw, swore softly.

"I can see now what he's up to. He's using the Stark boy to get you."

"I can't let them punish Danny, even if he did what they claim. I don't have any choice—"

"The boy's not guilty of anything," Reno said, motioning the woman to silence. "Laymon, the rancher he works for, says Danny never left his place all that morning, so it couldn't have been him. Says he's got witnesses who'll swear to it."

Lucilla's face had brightened as Magatagan's words registered on her mind. "Then Danny—he won't have to be tried? It was all a mistake—"

"Not a mistake," Reno said. "Was a scheme of Wagner's to force you into seeing things his way. I'm riding out to see him right away, let him know we've got proof that the Stark boy didn't have anything to do with what he's charging him with—if it ever happened at all—and that I want him turned loose."

There were tears in Lucilla Roth's eyes as she suddenly moved close to Magatagan and threw her arms around him.

"Oh, Reno, I'm so relieved! I had given up, made

up my mind to do what Bart Wagner wanted, and
then you—''

"Can forget about him, and when I'm done, he
won't ever bother you again.''

She drew back slightly. ''Do you think he'll let
Danny go?''

"Hard to say how he'll react, but if he tells me no,
I'll figure out some other way, one short of—''

A spate of gunshots echoed through the morning
hush. Magatagan turned at once and started for the
door.

"Trouble. Best I see what it is,'' he said, and
hurried out onto the street.

22

A dozen or more men were on the porch in front of the Bull's Head. He could see the glint of weapons, and it was plain there had been a shoot-out—one involving soldiers, for the blue of uniforms was in evidence. Elsewhere the street had cleared, those who had been moving along it for one purpose or another having taken cover for fear of being struck by stray bullets.

Grim, angered by what he knew he would be facing, Magatagan headed for the Bull's Head at a run. When he drew near, he recognized two of the men on the saloon's porch: Jed Bleeker, and one who had been in Rand's office at the time he'd served notice on the Bull's Head owner to get rid of his gunmen. There were four soldiers, two of whom were lying in the dust—either dead or badly wounded, for neither was moving.

Magatagan, gun in hand, reached the end of the porch. Bleeker, backed by four of his friends—evidently more of Rand's hard-case bullies who had ignored the order to move on—were facing two soldiers standing beside the pair who had been shot.

"Go ahead," Bleeker was taunting them. "Just like to see if you're any better at shooting than them pals of your'n."

"Back off, Bleeker!" Reno called sharply, coming in to the porch from its end.

The squat gunman whirled in surprise. His eyes narrowed as his mouth snapped shut. The pistol in his hand came up in a swift arc, stopped abruptly as Magatagan's weapon blasted the taut silence. Bleeker staggered back, began to fall.

The men with Bleeker had all wheeled with the squat gunman. As Jed went down, the one next to him made a stab for his pistol. Reno's .44 roared again. The outlaw threw wide his arms, spun, and collapsed across Bleeker's lifeless body.

Then, with the echoes rolling along the buildings lining the street, Magatagan faced the remaining gunmen.

"Your choice," he said in a soft voice. "Draw— or get on your horses and ride out."

There was a moment of uncertainty among the three, and then all pivoted and moved off the porch, walking in a stiff, hurried way toward the corral at the rear of the saloon.

"There's another dead man inside, Marshal," one of the soldiers said. "Was a whiskey drummer. Bleeker shot him too."

Magatagan nodded. "Get in there and drag him out," he said, reloading his pistol as he started for the Bull's Head's entrance. "Warned Rand—told him to get rid of that bunch, too. Seems he paid no mind. Best thing now is to clean out the place—for good."

Stepping purposefully into the saloon, Reno glanced about. He caught a glimpse of Monty Rand hurrying out the back. There were no customers, only Pete the bartender and several girls in sight.

"You've got five minutes to get your stuff and

clear out!'' he shouted, and fired a bullet into the shelf of bottled whiskey on the back bar.

At the shot, the clatter of breaking glass, and the trickling sound of spilling liquor, Pete rushed out from behind the counter, and dodging past the two soldiers removing the body of the drummer, he made a run for the door. Screams had arisen from the women, some of whom were hurrying toward the rear entrance of the building while others scurried for the front.

Magatagan, standing before the counter, sent another bullet into the stock of bottled liquor, filling the building again with deafening echoes, smoke, and the renewed clatter of shattering glass. A yell came from the upper floor; a man, with one of the girls, appeared. Both hastily descended the stairs.

''What the hell's going on?''

Reno ignored the question. ''Anybody else up there?'' he asked the girl.

''No—don't think so,'' she replied, features stiff with fright, and with her male companion, she hurried on.

Reno, holstering his pistol, dug into a vest pocket for a match. Scratching it into life on the counter, he stepped in close, waited until the small flame was at its strongest, and then flipped it into the pool of liquor on the floor behind the bar. The alcohol caught instantly, sent flames roaring upward. Dropping back, Magatagan waited until the fire had spread to the adjacent walls and was licking hungrily at the ceiling; then he retreated to the street where a swelling crowd was gathering.

Cheers and catcalls greeted him as he emerged from the pall of smoke and heat, but he scarcely heard. Halting, he glanced around. In the jostling

assemblage he caught sight of Dolly Jo. She was
with three other girls who had worked in the saloon.
Dolly Jo returned his glance soberly and then turned
away. And then on beyond the burning structure he
saw Rand, with Pete and another man, racing off on
their horses.

Some of the anger within him faded, and moving
on into the cluster of people, all now falling back in
the face of the crackling fire's heat, Reno crossed to
where the two soldiers were crouched beside their
downed friends.

"Which one of you is O'Hanlon?"

At Magatagan's sharp, unyielding tone one of the
pair pointed to the figure stretched out in the dust
before him.

"That's the sarge. He's bad hit, and I reckon he
ain't got long. Bullet ripped out his innards."

Reno hunched beside the man, noting only then
the triple stripes on his sleeve. Reaching out, he
shook the soldier.

"O'Hanlon, this is the marshal! Listen to me."

The noncom opened his eyes wearily. A frown
knotted his weathered features.

"I'm asking you about that boy you put in the
guardhouse for the major," Magatagan continued.
"He's innocent, ain't he?"

O'Hanlon's frown deepened, but he made no reply.

Reno brushed off a live spark that fell on the soldier,
and shook him again—this time more vigorously.

"You're dying, Sergeant, and that boy could die,
too, unless you tell the truth. He didn't have anything
to do with that woman, did he?"

O'Hanlon did not respond for a long minute and
then shook his head. "No—"

An angry mutter came from the men near enough
to hear what was being said.

"Wagner had you fix it up with that woman
to accuse the boy so you could put him in the
guardhouse."

O'Hanlon's head moved slightly, signifying that
such was true.

"The whole damned thing was a frame-up, a scheme
of Major Wagner's to get something he wanted—"

Reno did not mention that Lucilla was the object
of the officer's plan. He could see no need to bring
her name into it, although eventually such would come
to light.

"That was the way of it, wasn't it?"

"Yeh," O'Hanlon managed in a gusty voice.
"Didn't want—to—do—it, but the—major—he—"

"It's all right," Reno said, coming to his feet. The
Bull's Head was now a seething mass of flames that
was driving the crowd farther back along the street.
He turned to the men close by.

"You heard what O'Hanlon said. I'll say it again
for you who didn't. Danny Stark's not guilty of
doing anything wrong. Wagner ordered the sergeant
to frame the boy and put him in the guardhouse at the
fort. He aims to hold a trial in the morning—before a
military court."

"No—like hell he will!" a voice shouted. "It's
about time we showed that goddamn bunch they
don't own this town!"

"They had no right grabbing the boy in the first
place. He weren't no soldier!"

"What are you going to do, Marshal?"

Reno shook his head. "Not sure how Wagner will
take it when he finds out we know what he was up
to—"

"The hell with that! I say we go get Danny!"

Magatagan raised both hands in an effort to silence the frenzied crowd. "That'd mean a lot of you would get shot—killed—"

"Why don't we let them have their damned trial, only we'll all be there to tell what the sergeant said?"

Magatagan was having the same thought, but he quickly discarded it. Bart Wagner was an unstable man; failing to accomplish his purpose—that of forcing Lucilla Roth to become his camp follower—he could proceed at once with a trial, have him found guilty and executed in hopes of saving face.

"I'm afraid that wouldn't work either," he said, brushing at his sleeve. The smoke hanging over the street was now so thick it was beginning to choke, and sparks were continuing to fall.

"Then how—"

"Want you to set tight—leave it up to me," Reno answered, falling back on the same tack he'd taken with Laymon.

He had to prevent the bloodshed that certainly would result if the men of the town went storming into Fort Shafter, armed and determined to release Danny Stark by force. And, too, Magatagan was considering himself. Twice now he'd broken the promise he had made to himself—that he'd not use his gun on any man again—and now he was being faced with the prospect of having to lead a vengeful posse on a raid that could only end with him killing once more.

"Won't anything happen to the boy—I give you my word on that," Reno continued. "But I'm needing something from you—your promise that you won't try doing something for him on your own."

A scatter of protest as well as agreement ran through

the crowd. Finally a voice said, "All right, Marshal, you're calling the shots, but we for damn sure ain't standing for them soldiers trying that boy!"

"Not when he ain't done nothing!"

Again Magatagan raised his hands for quiet. "Go on about your business," he said. "Soon as I get my plan worked out, I'll send word, and we can get together at the jail. That good enough for you?"

"Good enough," several voices replied.

23

Magatagan, without the faintest idea in mind of
how he could free Danny Stark and avoid bloodshed,
and wishing to avoid any more questions concerning
the matter, turned and headed back to his office. The
crowd, he noticed, did not immediately start to break
up, as he hoped. Instead the men continued to stand
around in small groups talking, while others began to
probe about the edges of the Bull's Head's smolder-
ing ruins.

Reno was digging deep into his mind for a way to
get Stark out of the fort's guardhouse and free of Bart
Wagner's control. He had to come up with something; the town, already at dangerous odds with the
army, was working itself up to a lynch-mob frenzy
over what Wagner had done, and it would take very
little to light the fuse that would send an armed party
of men out to Fort Shafter determined to release
Danny.

Such could result only in bloodshed and failure.
No matter how disorganized and undermanned the
post was, the soldiers there would have the advantage
and would more than hold their own.

He'd go see Wagner once more, Reno decided as
he entered his office, and do his best to reason with
the officer. Perhaps Wagner—despite his pride and

the streak of instability that was apparent at times—
when told that proof of the boy's innocence and the
purpose behind his being framed was known, would
back down and order the boy released.

Deep within himself Magatagan realized there was
small chance of that. Wagner, being the kind of man
he was and even knowing full well he was wrong,
would never admit it. The officer would find grounds
of some sort upon which to proceed with Danny
Stark's trial; and being the post commander, the few
soldiers on hand, however undisciplined, would obey
him.

Reno moved restlessly about inside the small room,
now close with the morning's heat. He wished now
he'd never laid eyes on Lucilla Roth and had not
given in and accepted the job as Lynchburg's marshal—
however temporary. He should have continued riding
as he'd planned and not played the role of the Good
Samaritan to a town that likely would lose its quarrel
with the government and be compelled to abandon
itself.

But he had taken on the chore, and he was never a
man to go back on a promise. He had already ac-
complished something—ridding the settlement of
Monty Rand and his saloon as well as Jed Bleeker
and the other outlaws who made the place their
hangout.

Not that in doing so he was putting an end to such
enterprises, Reno admitted wryly to himself as he sat
down to the rolltop. Like as not, Cal Beatty—human
nature being what it was—at that very moment was
busy arranging for Dolly Jo Morrison and the other
women who had worked for Rand at the Bull's Head
to throw in their lot with him at his saloon.

Cal Beatty, a businessman, would probably begin
enlarging his premises immediately to accommodate
the surge of additional patronage he was certain to
enjoy since he would be the master of the only
enterprise of that nature in Lynchburg. And with the
fulfillment of such, the settlement's attendant problem could start again—all depending on the size of
Cal Beatty's greed.

But it would be of no concern to him, Magatagan
thought. He would be gone by then, and it would be
up to another lawman to keep things in order. Meantime, he was faced with a problem of his own—what
to do about Danny Stark without letting the situation
turn into wholesale bloodshed.

Reno glanced toward the street as the sound of
walking horses reached him. Three soldiers, one wearing bandages on his shoulder, were moving by; a
fourth man, hung across his saddle, his animal at the
end of a short lead rope, brought up the rear of the
procession as it headed out the road to Shafter. There
would be a fresh grave in the post cemetery by
sundown that day—thanks to Jeb Bleeker.

An idea came suddenly to Reno. He'd ride out to
the post, see Wagner as planned, and failing to accomplish anything—which he frankly anticipated—he'd
then return to town and let matters slide until night.
Then, with three or four men of the kind he felt he
could rely on to do exactly as he said, he would
return to the fort and, under cover of darkness, make
their way to the guardhouse and set Danny Stark
free.

He'd take careful note of the building's location
while he was there, paying particular attention also to
how well patrolled it was—if at all. Thus no time

would be lost once he and the men with him were inside the fort. It should be no big problem, for most of the soldiers garrisoned there were absent, and under Major Wagner, clearly no stickler for regulations, there likely would be no sentries on duty.

A plan for helping Danny Stark now complete and firmly fixed in his mind, Magatagan rose, crossed to the doorway of his office, and stared off down the street. There were still a dozen or so persons moving about the smoky remainder of the Bull's Head, evidently searching for items of value. A number of horses were now picketed at the rack in front of Beatty's—an indication that business had already picked up considerably for him. As there were no signs of Dolly Jo and the other girls who had worked for Rand, Reno supposed they were already inside the saloon, doing business as usual.

Stepping out into the bright sunshine and thinking of nothing else to do for the moment, Reno went directly to Phil Perkins' Restaurant, where he settled the tab for the breakfasts provided the two soldiers—a dollar even covering both, according to Perkins. The amount was too reasonable to be correct, Magatagan knew, but he supposed the restaurant man wanted to do his part for the good of the town, and accordingly let it pass.

That taken care of, Reno returned to the street, made a slow patrol of its length, all the while endeavoring to decide the best time to pay his call on Wagner. Around noon had been a good time before, and it should be again. It was getting close to that hour now, he realized. He'd drop by Beatty's, get himself a drink, and then make the ride to Fort Shafter.

The saloon was well-attended. Of only average size, two dozen patrons were enough to crowd it, but no one seemed to mind that, for almost twice that number were present and the constant laughter and drone of conversation indicated that everyone there was enjoying himself.

Nodding to those who spoke to him, as well as a few men who regarded him resentfully, Magatagan shouldered his way to the short bar, which was lined with patrons. Beatty was alone behind the counter, his face red and shining with sweat, and when he saw Reno, he grinned broadly and hurried up.

"Welcome, Marshal! I reckon you can see what you done for me! Now, anything you want's on the house."

"Whiskey," Magatagan said, returning the coin he'd taken from a pocket to its place.

Beatty set a tumbler-size glass of liquor on the counter before Reno and, still smiling happily, glanced around.

"Going to have to build onto the place—sure need more room. Got to have room for gambling and dancing. The girls need somewhere to put up, too."

Magatagan studied his whiskey thoughtfully. Then, "You going to rename it the Bull's Head!" he asked dryly.

Beatty's face sobered as he caught Reno's meaning. "No, sir, Marshal! I ain't going to be running nothing like Monty Rand did. My place'll be straight and decent. I ain't letting no cardsharps hang around and I won't be needing no pistoleers either—not the kind of saloon I aim to be running."

"Glad to hear that . . . Obliged for the drink,"

Magatagan said, and finishing his liquor, he made his way back through the crowd to the street.

Bending his steps again toward his office, Reno slowed as the rapid beat of an approaching horse, coming in from the direction of the fort, drew his attention. Moments later the rider burst into view. Surprise rolled through Magatagan; it was the boy he'd seen Sergeant O'Hanlon leading into the fort—Danny Stark.

"Marshal!" the boy shouted when he saw Magatagan, and veering course when he reached the street, he angled for the lawman.

Others in nearby buildings heard Stark's yell and hurried into the open. Reno, relieved but puzzled by Danny's appearance, and wondering how it came to pass, moved forward to meet him.

"They turned me loose!" Danny said as he brought his lathered horse to a stop. "A couple of them soldiers—"

"Not the major?" Magatagan said, frowning.

"Nope, he wasn't around, I heard one of them say. They just come up, opened the guardhouse door, and told me to get. Had my horse waiting right there for me."

Two soldiers. It could have been the pair he'd jailed and then fed that morning, returning what they figured was a favor; or perhaps it was two of the three men who survived the shoot-out with Bleeker and his hard-case friends. They would have had time to reach Shafter and accomplish the act.

Undoubtedly it had been them, Magatagan decided. They had heard what O'Hanlon had to say about Stark being framed, and knowing Bart Wagner first-hand, they had taken steps to prevent what would have been nothing less than murder. Too, they also could have been repaying a favor—one that likely had saved their lives.

The problem of getting Danny out of Shafter's guardhouse was now resolved. Reno reckoned he need worry no longer about that, but aware of Bart Wagner's turn of mind, he was equally certain the matter was far from over.

"Expect you'd best keep out of sight," he said to the boy. "Ride by Mrs. Roth's, let her and Abby know you're all right, then head out to Laymon's. You'll be safe there."

Danny frowned. "You think they'll come after me again?"

"If the major wasn't the one who turned you loose, you can bet on it. Soon as he finds out you're gone, he'll be down here with as many men as he can mount looking for you."

Stark shook his head. "I reckon I'd better wait right here, then. I sure didn't do any of them things they said I did, so there ain't no need for me to hide. I'm man enough to stand up to—"

"That'd be the thing to do if you were dealing with somebody besides Wagner. He can only see things his way. . . . Now, ride on out of here, leave the major to me."

Danny hesitated for several moments, and then wheeling his horse about, he started up the street in the direction of Lucilla Roth's house at a quick trot.

Magatagan waited until the boy was gone from view, and then turned to face the half-dozen or so persons who had come into the open at the sound of Stark's arrival.

"I'll be obliged if you folks will get back inside your places and stay there," he said. "Could be trouble coming and I don't want any of you hurt."

Not waiting to see if his request was followed, Reno continued on his way to his office, and there took up a stand in the doorway. Wagner would come there first, he was sure.

☆ 24 ☆

Magatagan did not have long to wait. Within minutes after he had taken up a stand in the doorway of his office, he heard the hard, fast hammer of horses on the road from Fort Shafter. And then shortly after that, Bart Wagner, accompanied by four cavalrymen, thundered into the street.

Reining in sharply, the officer glanced along the buildings, all of which appeared deserted at that moment. He caught sight of Magatagan at that point, immediately spurred his mount toward the lawman.

"Where's that boy?" he demanded, stirring up dust as he pulled his horse to a sliding stop in front of Reno. "I want him."

Magatagan, lank figure slack against the doorframe of the office, shrugged. "Forget it, Major. He's not guilty of—"

"I'll decide if he's guilty or not!" Wagner snapped. Turning his head slightly, he watched Lige Crow trotting up, shotgun in one hand, from the nearby stable. "You got him locked in that jail?"

"That's where he'd be if there's was any truth in what you charged him with. Happens I know—"

"You don't know anything about it," Wagner shouted, his face ruddy and glistening with sweat. The officer was in full uniform, even to saber.

146

"I'm here to take him back for trial. Now, I warn you, Marshal—you had better turn him over to me! I have the men and the authority to take him by force, if necessary."

Lige Crow had moved in beside Magatagan, now stood with shotgun hanging in the crook of an arm, only a stride away. Elsewhere along the roadway separating Lynchburg's business buildings people were appearing, but mindful of Reno's warning—and of past experience—were keeping close to their doorways in the event gunplay erupted.

"Don't try it, Wagner," Magatagan said evenly. "This town don't belong to you—and you better get over the idea that it does."

Wagner's eyes flashed as anger rose to greater heights within him. "Just who the goddamn hell do you think you are, talking to me like that? This town's under military control—my control—and what I say is law!"

The officer paused for breath, and then, voice rising hysterically, added, "If I decide I want this town wiped off the map—burned to the ground—I can do it. I have the power to say whether it lives or dies! You hear that, Marshal? I can kill it—let it die—and right now I'm thinking of doing just that!"

The troopers ranged in a half-circle behind Bart Wagner stirred uncomfortably in their saddles, some looking down, others turning their eyes to the lower end of the street and the still-smoking embers of the Bull's Head.

"Maybe so," Reno said calmly, wanting to stand firm in the interests of the town, but aware of Wagner's uncertain temperament, hoping not to set the officer off on a wild burst of anger that could result in bloodshed.

"I'm telling you again!" Wagner raged. "Where's that boy? I want him! He's got to stand trial for—"

"Major, we know the whole story," Magatagan cut in, beginning to weary of the continual wrangling. "Best you and your soldiers turn around and go back to the fort. There won't be any trial."

In the hush that followed Magatagan's quiet words the far-off moaning of a dove rode clearly through the hot, motionless air. Mouth working convulsively, Wagner stared at Reno, one hand clutching the hilt of his saber suggestively.

"What do you mean by that, sir?" he demanded, his tone now icy polite.

"Just this. I know—the whole town knows—that you had that boy picked up and taken to your guardhouse on a trumped-up charge. You wanted to use him to force a certain lady to see things your way."

"That's a lie—a goddamn lie!" Wagner screamed. "The boy is guilty! I have a woman who will—"

"Wasting your breath, Major. Sergeant O'Hanlon told us the straight of it—something I'd already pretty well figured out. He told us what you had him do in front of witnesses—some of your own men, in fact."

"Damn them!" Wagner shouted. "I know there's them who've been going behind my back—and I know who they are, just as I know who it was that let that boy escape this morning. I'm going to make them pay for it! I'm the commanding officer at that fort, and they're going to obey my orders or I'll have the hide flayed from their backs!"

Sweat was dripping from Bart Wagner's face, and a wildness filled his eyes when he finished his tirade. A soldier wearing the chevrons of a corporal kneed his horse forward a few paces.

"Major, I think we best—" he began, but the officer cut him off abruptly.

"I'll take no advice from the ranks!" he declared, and spurred his mount in closer to Magatagan and Lige Crow. "You handing that boy over to me or not?"

Magatagan shrugged. "Fact is, I couldn't if I was of a mind to. I don't know exactly where he is—"

Wagner's eyes narrowed, and a slyness filled them. "I can find him—don't you think I can't. This town's not so big that I can't ferret him out. You're just trying to sucker me, make a fool of me."

"No, just telling you to forget about Danny Stark and not to go looking for him."

"See! I'm right! You know where he's hiding. Proves you're hand in glove with him!"

"Told you I didn't know where he was right now— and I meant it."

"What about you—you there with the shotgun," Wagner demanded, abruptly turning to Crow. "You know where that boy's hiding?"

"Sure don't," the stableman drawled after cutting loose with a spurt of tobacco juice that sent small geysers of dust into the air when it hit. "I ain't got no idea a'tall."

"You're both liars!" Wagner yelled. "I've a mind to take you back to the fort and have the truth flogged out of you—make you tell—"

"Do you no good," Magatagan said, shifting restlessly, wishing the senseless bickering would come to an end. "I don't know where Stark is. Neither does Lige, and I'm tired of talking about it."

"I'm not leaving here until—"

"Besides, you've no reason to want him. I've told you everybody in town and likely every man out at

the fort knows it was a frame-up. Leave the boy
alone. Your scheme didn't work. Best you forget the
whole thing.''

"Never!" Wagner yelled. "You're defying the
United States army, and I won't allow that! Corporal,
put these men under arrest and take them to the
guardhouse.''

The noncom frowned, glanced about, a helpless
sort of look on his sun-reddened features. "But, sir, I
can't—''

"You're with them, too!" the officer shouted.
"You're one of them against me! All right, goddamn
you, I'll handle it myself!''

In a sudden move Wagner was off his horse and on
the ground. As his booted feet hit solidly, he whipped
out the pistol hanging at his side.

"Now maybe you'll listen to me!" he declared,
and triggered the weapon.

Neither Magatagan nor Lige Crow had expected
the officer to shoot. As the blast rocked the silence
and the bullet tore into the wood facing of the doorway only inches from Reno's head, the lawman instinctively drew his weapon and fired. At such close
range, the heavy .44 slug driving into Bart Wagner's
chest knocked the man back against his horse. The
startled animal shied away, leaving the officer hanging motionless, half-bent, pistol pointed at the ground,
for a long breath. And then, a frown twisting his
agonized face, he collapsed.

Magatagan—taut, attention centered now on the
cavalrymen, uncertain in mind how they would react—
silently rode out the dragging moments that followed.
And then the corporal, shaking his head, dismounted
and stepped up beside the man who had been his
commanding officer.

"Sure sorry about this, Marshal," he said, "but the major ain't been just right in the head for some time. If it's all right with you, we'll take him back to the post and see to burying him."

The tension gripping Magatagan faded. He nodded, noting, as he did, people hurrying up along the street from all directions—among them Lucilla Roth.

"Go ahead, Corporal," he said. "I'm plenty sorry it came down to this, too. There somebody at the fort who can taken command until the colonel returns?"

"Yes, sir, Captain Agnew. Been on maneuvers, but he's expected in today. He can take over," the noncom replied, beckoning to one of the men with him. Together they lifted the slack form of Bart Wagner and hung it across his saddle. Securing it, both men mounted and prepared to ride out. The corporal hesitated, looked back at Reno.

"Ain't sure how this'll turn out, Marshal," he said. "Was plain you had to do what you did, but it all happening on an army reservation—"

"We're not sure of that, Corporal—"

"Yeh, maybe not, but if there's a court, me and the boys with me'll speak up the truth."

Magatagan felt an arm slip under his, and looked around. It was Lucilla. She was smiling and relief filled her eyes.

"Obliged to you," Reno said attention again on the corporal, "but you won't have to bother. I don't expect to be around long."

The soldier said no more, but rode on with the other cavalrymen. Lige Crow broke the silence that followed.

"I hear you right? You're already moving on?"

Lucilla's fingers tightened about Magatagan's arm. He nodded. "Best thing for me to do. This shooting will be looked into, and with my reputation, being in the right won't make one whit's difference. The law will hold me responsible.''

John Broome pushed to the fore of the crowd gathered in front of the marshal's office.

"I expect we'll all have something to say about that—but I reckon you're right. The army ain't going to look kindly on what you did—them still claiming the town's on military property—and like you say, the law's got their mind made up about you before they ever get here.''

"Don't like moving on," Reno said, tightening his arm to draw Lucilla closer. "Found a good reason to stay—several, in fact—but I know when I'm in a losing game. Real sorry nobody turned up to be my deputy, who could now take over the job," he added, surrendering the marshal's badge to Broome.

"We'll find somebody," the merchant said. "Town's in good shape on account of you. Won't be no hard chore finding a man to wear your star now. . . . When you aim to leave?"

"Probably first light tomorrow morning—"

"Good. That'll give me time to talk to the rest of the council. I want to see you get a full month's pay for the job you've done.''

"Appreciate that. Couple of things I have to see to myself before I go—"

"You ain't going nowhere!" a voice declared from beyond the crowd.

Magatagan raised his glance to see who the speaker might be. A long sigh slipped from his lips. The rifleman on the sorrel had caught up with him.

☆ 25 ☆

The crowd parted quickly, leaving a clear aisle between Magatagan and the rider standing with rifle ready in his arms. Reno considered the man coolly while he disengaged his arm from Lucilla's and eased slowly away from her.

"Lay that scatter-gun down on the ground, Grandpa," the rider directed, nodding at Lige Crow. "And if any of the rest of you people got some ideas about horning in, forget it, because I sure don't want to hurt you. This here's between the killer and me."

In the tense hush that had settled over the crowd, Magatagan shrugged, smiled bleakly. "I take it your name's Bigbee—or maybe I best say Locklear, and you're some relation to Henry—"

"Right. I'm Will Locklear, and it was my pa you shot down. I'm here to make you pay for doing it."

Magatagan's mouth tightened into a wry grimace. The chain of vengeance was a never-ending thing; each killing gave birth to another.

"Best you know the story before you make your move. I killed you pa because he killed mine. Way I see it, we're even."

153

Locklear was quiet for a long breath. Then, "You can't get me to swallow that—"

"I don't much give a damn whether you believe it or not, but that's the way it was. Took me a lot of years to track down your pa. Changing his name like he did made it tough for me."

Will Locklear shook his head. "Name's always been Locklear. Never heard of no Henry Bigbee until you came along."

Understanding came to Reno. Bigbee had been a false name all along, he realized. The man had lied from the start—from the very day he had persuaded Dave Magatagan to throw in with him. But that was neither here nor there, and changed nothing but a glimpse of the past.

"Doesn't matter," Magatagan said. "Best we both forget it."

"Not about to!" Locklear snapped. "Seen you draw on that soldier. Real fast with your iron—I've got to admit that. But I expect I'm just as quick with this rifle."

Locklear raised the weapon slightly for Reno to see. The stock had been cut off about a third of its length, and the barrel had been shortened, making it easier to maneuver.

"You won't stand a chance," Magatagan said quietly. "Not bragging, just giving you the facts. I can leather my gun and still kill you before you get off a shot."

A flicker of uncertainty crossed Locklear's face. He frowned, glanced about, moisture shining on his cheeks. John Broome stepped forward.

"He's telling you the truth, boy. He'll kill you sure. And there's been enough blood spilled. I want you to put down that rifle and forget what you come here for."

Several other men moved in closer to Reno, making it clear they shared Broome's sentiments. Lige Crow calmly reached down and retrieved his shotgun. At that Will Locklear's shoulders sagged. A heavy sigh escaped him.

"All right, I'll believe what you said about my pa and yours. I'm willing to call it quits."

Magatagan felt Lucilla again at his side, heard a murmur of relief run through the crowd.

"You done the smart thing, Locklear," Broome said. "Time for killing is finished. You want to shake the marshal's hand?"

Locklear gave that brief thought and shook his head. "No, reckon not—just let it go like it is. No matter how you look at it, he killed my pa—and it wouldn't be right if I accepted him as a friend. I'm just hoping I can stand by my word and not throw down on him next time we meet."

"Not much chance of that," Broome said. "He's riding out in the morning. Like as not you'll never see him again."

"And I'll be going with him," Lucilla Roth said, looking up hopefully at Reno. Ignoring the surprised crowd, she added, "If he'll have me."

"Have you!" Magatagan echoed. "You already know the answer to that. I'd like nothing more—had even maybe hoped a little—but how can you? You've got your daughter, and there's your home and all the things you have—"

"Abby's marrying Danny Stark tonight, and I'm turning my house and everything else over to them. I've nothing to keep me here—and I'm tired of my kind of life. I want to go with you."

Ignoring the intently listening and watching people surrounding them, Magatagan put his arm around Lucilla and drew her close. "I won't have anything much to offer—leastwise not for a while."

"A while's soon enough," she said happily.